T

NO GOLD WHEN YOU GO

In five centuries, Seldon's Gold had travelled far. Kings and cut-throats, freemen and freebooters, all had chased it. Toots McKern definitely had an ancient coin in his pocket when they fished him from the bay. A wealthy collector hired Mark Preston to locate the treasure. Preston rated his chances low, particularly when he found how many people wanted to stop him. He had to move and think even faster than usual to keep out of his two least favourite places — jail and the morgue.

PETER CHAMBERS

NO GOLD WHEN YOU GO

Complete and Unabridged

LINFORD
Leicester

First published in Great Britain in 1966

First Linford Edition
published 2004

British Library CIP Data

Chambers, Peter, *1924* –
    No gold when you go.—Large print ed.—
Linford mystery library
    1. Private investigators—Fiction
    2. Detective and mystery stories
    3. Large type books
    I. Title
823.9′14 [F]

ISBN 1–84395–270–X

Published by
F. A. Thorpe (Publishing)
Anstey, Leicestershire

Set by Words & Graphics Ltd.
Anstey, Leicestershire
Printed and bound in Great Britain by
T. J. International Ltd., Padstow, Cornwall

before

The dark police sedan sped smoothly through the deserted town. Sergeant Gil Randall of Homicide stared sourly out at the empty streets. At five in the morning a man had a right to be almost anywhere else on earth in preference to heading for the morgue. Beside him, hands jammed deep in his overcoat pockets Captain Rourke sat bolt upright, eyes fixed unwinkingly on the nape of the driver's neck. He was thinking hard too, but not about his bad luck in taking the call. Instead he was almost looking forward to the case. It had been almost a month since Monkton City had needed the Homicide Detail, and the big Irishman was not a man to relish inactivity.

The car drew to a smooth halt outside the rectangular gray building. There were lights at the rear and the two men clambered out and headed for the side

1

entrance. They were both big men, but next to Randall, the Captain looked only average size. The sergeant was built like the side of a barn, and usually moved ponderously. But if he had to, he could be quick and light on his feet as a ballet dancer, as many a law-breaker had learned too late. They had also found the heavy sleepy face to be a poor pointer to the rapier mind behind it.

Rourke was different. Fifteen years older than Randall, his tough grizzled face left people in no doubt about the calibre of man they were dealing with. Honest, tough and intelligent was the verdict, and the verdict was right. The two officers with their contrasting styles were one of the most efficient combinations in the state, and as any member of the criminal fraternity knew, if the two R's were looking for you, best take a fast train out.

The side door was open. As they went in an elderly man emerged from a small cubicle, yawning prodigiously and scratching at a white head.

'Mornin', gents,' he greeted. 'Coroner's

men have your customer in number three.'

They nodded thanks and walked between immaculate white walls to a glass-panelled door marked '3'. A group of men looked round at the newcomers. Rourke looked at a tubby balding man with steel-rimmed spectacles.

'Dixon,' he greeted. 'You know Randall.'

'Sure,' was the reply. 'How are you? This here is Kemp from my office.'

Randall looked enquiringly at the third man. He was a middle-aged outdoor looking man in a thick seaman's jersey and thigh boots.

'My name is Nye,' said the seaman. 'Benjamin Nye. I found him.'

'Name is Rourke,' barked the Irishman. 'I'm from Homicide, Mr. Nye. Like to hear all about it.'

Nye looked beseechingly at Dixon, who pretended not to notice.

'Again? I have to go through it again?'

'I'm afraid you do. Start at the beginning.'

The bronzed man shrugged.

'Nothing much to it. I was out off Penlee Sound, doing a little night fishing — '

'Alone?'

'Certainly alone,' was the surprised reply. 'When I go out for those big fellas I don't want any chatterbox with me.'

'All right. So you were fishing.'

'I heard this launch, see — '

'How'd you know it was a launch?' interrupted Randall. 'It was dark.'

The fisherman looked pained.

'Now look,' he said slowly, 'I want to co-operate with you people. But if we're going to get along, we have to get something straight. I have been on and around the sea for more'n thirty years. There isn't a whole hell of a lot I don't know about the sea, the fish, and the vessels. If I say it was a launch, you can put your pension on it. Am I getting through?'

Rourke grinned quickly and turned to Randall.

'We'll take it as a launch, sergeant. Go on Mr. Nye.'

Nye was mollified, and now addressed

4

himself to the captain.

'Well, sir, I heard this launch — ' he emphasised the word and looked triumphantly at Randall — 'and I looked around for it. Now that was the first thing struck me as odd. It didn't have any lights.'

'Ah,' said Rourke with satisfaction. 'What time was this, Mr. Nye?'

'I didn't actually check the time then, not right at that minute. But I wrote it down in my mind most careful a while later. It was then ten minutes to four. So I estimate the launch was out there around three-thirty.'

'Good, good. You heard the launch. Then what?'

'Like I said, the first strange thing was, no lights. I mean the thing made me mad enough coming out there in the first place — '

Rourke's eyebrows went up.

'Mad? Why would it do that, Mr. Nye?'

The fisherman snorted.

'I ain't saying you don't know your business, Mr. Rourke, but you sure's hell don't know nothing 'bout fish. I had been sitting up on top of that water more'n three hours. Just sitting there without even breathing very hard. Then up comes this thing making more noise'n a Fourth of July parade and you ask me why I'm mad? Why, every fish within miles would've — '

The captain held up a hand.

'I get the picture. Some day we'll have a long talk about fishing. Right now let's stay with the launch.'

'Well, I'm standing there, straining my eyes to try to catch sight of the thing. Wasn't too much of a moon, you know. Then I seen it, between me and the shore. Not more'n a couple hundred yards away.'

'So they must have seen your lights?' asked Randall.

Nye shook his head.

'Not necessarily. I was broadside on to them, and I wasn't showing nothing but minimum regulation lights. Them fish ain't blind, you know. Then the launch stops, and I hear this splash.'

'Big splash?'

'Big enough. Remember, I hadn't

heard a human soul so much as breathe in three hours. My ears were kind of tuned up. Anyway, there's this splash. Then the launch turns around and heads back.'

'Heads back which way?'

Again the fisherman shook his head.

'I got good eyes and good ears, but I couldn't tell you that on a dark night.'

'What happened then?'

'I was nosey, you might say. So far as catching any fish went, I knew that was a busted flush now these people had made all that noise. So I thought I'd take a look, see if I could spot what they'd dumped. I started up my motor and went over to where I'd seen the launch. There's a small searchlight on the *Starfish* — '

' — name of his boat,' cut in Dixon.

' — and I fooled around for twenty minutes or so. Then I saw this thing floating. When I got up close I could see it was a man. I pulled him in and headed in here just as fast as I could.'

'This man was dead?' barked Rourke.

'Oh, he was dead all right.'

'Did you recognise him?'

'No, sir. Never laid eyes on him before.'

Rourke nodded thoughtfully.

'Thank you, Mr. Nye, you've been a great help. We may want to have another talk with you later. Meantime, if you'll just make a statement of what you've told me, we won't bother you any more for now. Just wait a few minutes, please.'

Nye looked pleased. The one named Rourke may not know much about fishing but he knew how to speak to a man.

The captain looked at Dixon.

'All right, Sam. Let's take a look at him.'

Dixon looked uncomfortable.

'They have him on the table, John.'

Rourke's face went hard.

'They what?'

The coroner's man took him by the arm.

'Let's just step into the corridor a moment.'

They went out. Randall and Kemp exchanged glances but didn't speak. Outside, Rourke turned round quickly.

'I'm surprised at you, Sam. You know

the law as well as anybody, and better than most. I have the jurisdiction here. Nobody should have touched that body before I saw it. Now, I want an explanation. Make it short and make it very damned good.'

Dixon removed his eyeglasses and began to polish them furiously.

'I don't want to quarrel with you, John, but you're going to have to bend a little bit on this one.'

'Tell me why?' suggested Rourke nastily.

'Legally speaking, we don't any of us stand on very firm ground on this one. We're all going to have to watch our tongues, co-operate, and generally, try to get along.'

'This guy is in my territory, and I don't have to take crap from anybody,' snorted Rourke.

The tubby man shook his head.

'Wrong. The body was picked up out at Penlee Sound. That is almost seven miles out in the Pacific Ocean, John. If that cadaver belongs to anybody it's probably the International Maritime Commission.'

Rourke said a word, but Dixon ignored him.

'That's in the first place. In the second place, you could say maybe he wasn't killed out there. Maybe it was done on the mainland, and that would give us a right to make a noise.'

'Why that's obvious,' said Rourke impatiently. 'They took him out there to dump him, saw Nye's lights and panicked. So they heaved him over and beat it.'

'Maybe,' returned the other noncommitally. 'But where did they come from? And where did they beat it to? Could have been anywhere along this coast-line fifty miles either way. Maybe more. They could even have come from Baja California. We just don't know.'

'H'm.' Rourke ran a thick thumb along his jaw. 'And Nye just brought him here because he's a Monkton man, right?'

'Right. We're going to need a little soft treading, John. So don't let's start off with you and me fighting because I let the M.E. have him. There was nothing to see that isn't still there.'

10

The Irishman chewed on his lower lip for a long moment. Then he said,

'O.K., Sam, we'll tread easy. But it's my case now, as far as I'm concerned.'

The coroner's man shrugged.

'Have it your way. But remember what I said.'

'Let's go take a look at him.'

They went into the mortuary operating theatre. Two men were bending over the naked body of a large man, partially covered with a white sheet.

'You know Captain Rourke, doctor,' announced Dixon.

The medic nodded without looking up.

'What've we got, doc?' enquired Rourke.

'Quite a bit. I've only had him about twenty minutes, so there'll be more to come later. Take a look at him.'

Rourke moved round to where he could see the man's head. He had a heavy Italian face, with thick lips and a broad flattened nose. On one cheek were two thin white scars. There were no marks visible on the head or chest.

'Cause of death?'

'There are five .44 bullets on the table behind you. I took them out of his back.'

'H'm,' grunted Rourke. 'What else?'

'I make him forty, forty-five. Weight is one ninety three, height five ten. From the shape he's in, I'd say he had been active most of his life. The last few years he's been letting himself run to seed. There are good muscles here, which have seen plenty of work in their time, but they're overlaid with fat, which helps to bear out my idea. So do his hands. As you see they're the hands of a worker, yet they're soft and pale. He seems to be a bit of a problem. Looking at him, you'd think he was a man of no great intelligence, and yet he doesn't seem to do any work. Then the manicure, that's been a regular and expensive indulgence. His teeth too. Some of them seem to have been treated by a construction worker on his day off, yet the more recent work shows the very latest highly expensive methods.'

Rourke listened appreciatively.

'You ever need a job, doc, my squad'll be glad to see you any time.'

The doctor smiled.

'Oh, there'll be more. You realise we have a lot of tests and these will take time.'

'So far, so fine. Thanks.' Rourke turned to Dixon.

'Where's his stuff?'

'Next room.'

The saturated clothes had been laid flat on a metal table. Rourke fingered at the suit.

'You could tell just by looking at that guy he'd wear a fifty buck suit,' he muttered.

'Sure,' agreed Dixon. 'So what was he doing in this outfit? Not much left out of three hundred dollars, huh?'

'Not much. What do you make of him, Sam? I mean after what the doc said and everything?'

'You know how my mind works, John. I see a guy in a suit like that hauled out of the drink with four holes in his back. To me it says hoodlum.'

Rourke nodded glumly.

'I'll go for that on what we have so far. Could be a break. Maybe some other dumb cop somewhere waiting to hear where an old friend went. This all there was on the body?'

There wasn't much. One handkerchief, nail-file, a small pile of change.

'No wallet, no watch, no car-keys?'

'It's all right there on the table,' insisted Dixon.

'H'm. Maybe somebody didn't want us to know who this guy was.'

The Irishman picked up the loose coins and chinked them in his hands absently. Then he frowned and spread out his huge paw, sorting the pieces with thick fingers.

'Yeah, I noticed that,' Dixon chimed in. 'You'd wonder a guy in those clothes would carry a slug.'

Rourke dumped the other coins beside the handkerchief and held up the one which interested him. It was approximately the size of a quarter, but the circumference was not perfectly round.

'If this guy was a counterfeiter, that is one of the worst slugs I ever laid eyes on,' opined his companion. 'It ain't even properly round.'

'Hold on, Sam, this is no ordinary slug. Listen.'

He dropped it on the metal surface of the table and it gave off a clear, ringing sound. The two men looked at it again. It was almost black in colour and thinner than a newly minted quarter.

'This is no slug, Sam. I think it's something else, something we ought to know about.'

'Such as?'

'Who knows? A medallion maybe, or something like that. A good-luck piece? Let's get back in there.'

The puzzled Dixon tagged along behind as Rourke went up to the doctor.

'Doc, would you have a cleaning agent here?' he demanded. 'Like to clean up this thing some.'

The medical examiner looked briefly up.

'Sure. Try a solution of hydrochloric, but watch your fingers. Les, do you mind?'

The lab man fiddled with bottles at a side table, handed Rourke a phial and a swab of cotton waste.

'Take it easy with that stuff, Captain,' he warned.

Rourke gingerly tipped a small quantity of the solution on to the pad then dabbed at the metal. At first nothing happened except a faint stinging smell. He rubbed at the place, and now the black dissolved and became a deep bronze colour, which in turn became lighter.

'Hey,' said Dixon excitedly, 'there's some kind of picture on there, John. Look, there's a line, and over there that's something curved. Guess you were right at that. It is some kind of medal.'

Patiently, Rourke worked on the surface. Gradually the worst of the discoloration disappeared.

'It's kind of worn, but I think I can make out what it's supposed to be,' piped Dixon. 'It's like one of those guys in the field events, you know, like in the games. He's throwing that flat thing the way they do. You know the thing.'

'A discus,' murmured Rourke.

'Sure, that's what I said. A discus. It's some kind of medal. Hey, you don't suppose it could be a real Olympic medal, huh? Not too many of those around.'

'I guess it could be,' agreed the

Irishman. 'Anyway, it's something to work at.'

'Just a moment.'

The doctor's curiosity had got the better of him. He'd left what he was doing and joined the group.

'What do you think, doc? You ever seen one of these?'

The newcomer shook his head.

'Would you mind cleaning the other side, Captain?'

'Sure.'

Rourke began rubbing again. There was a faint but unmistakeable man's head on the back. Around the top of his head were marks.

'The hair ain't so hot,' contributed Dixon.

'That is not supposed to be hair, Mr. Dixon,' whispered the doctor. 'I can be wrong, very wrong on this. But I think those marks up there are leaves.'

'Leaves? On his head?' scorned the coroner's man.

Rourke looked at the doctor curiously.

'All right, doc. Let's say they are leaves. What does it give us?'

The doctor shook his head again, not anxious to commit himself.

'I'm just groping in my memory back to college days, Captain. I'd hate to set you off on a wild goose chase.'

'Doctor, I spend the greater part of my life chasing those geese. Let's have it.'

'Could I hold it?'

'Certainly.'

Rourke handed it over. The doctor stared at it, turned it over again and again.

'What was it you said, Mr. Dixon? An Olympic gold medal, wasn't it?'

'Yeah, but I was just tossing a ball around.'

The doctor smiled quietly.

'You'll never toss a better ball, Mr. Dixon. Unless I am very much mistaken, this an Olympic gold coin.'

'You mean medal, huh?'

'No. I mean coin. And I don't mean the Olympic Games you refer to. I think this is a gold coin that was struck when the first Olympic Games were held. The real ones.'

Rourke looked at the medic's serious face.

'Go on, Doctor.'

'Well, as I say, this is not a subject in which I am qualified. But look at the discus thrower on this side.'

'Aw come on, doc, look at Tokyo the other year. There was discus throwers everywhere you went. Souvenir medals, the works.'

The doctor looked at Dixon pityingly.

'Now look at the other side, please. It was the custom in Roman times to inscribe the head of Caesar on all gold coins. And those leaves appear on everything that carries Caesar's head. This little item, gentlemen, is the greater part of two thousand years old.'

Dixon said nothing, but his face was sceptical. Rourke, however, was impressed.

'Would it be valuable, Doctor?'

'Oh, certainly. Old coins are a cult, you know. I don't know anything about the market, but it will be easy enough for you to check.'

'That it will. I'm very obliged to you,

Doctor. Come on, Sam.'

Outside, the coroner's man whispered.

'You think there may be something in the doc's kooky theory?'

'I don't know, Sam. But it won't take long to check. If he's right, we have a beautiful lead.'

'How so?'

'These things are all catalogued. You don't just get 'em out of slot machines. There could have been a big steal, anywhere in the world. These old coins hold their value everywhere. Come on, we have a lot of work to do.'

Dixon shrugged, and followed him. Old coins, Roman emperors. Everybody was a little crazy at five thirty in the morning.

1

It was one of those big rambling houses they used to use a lot in the movies. It was four in the afternoon and the sun was beating down on the roof of the Chev as though it was trying to burn the whole thing into the gravelled drive. Apart from the fact it was making the shirt stick to my back, and the rest of me to the upholstery, the sun had no business around that house. It needed lightning and rain, a loose shutter banging crazily in the wind. It needed the darkness of night, an occasional moon shaft through the shifting clouds, a white dead face appearing momentarily at an upper window. There ought to be the silent swooping of vampire bats around the ragged trees, the sinister grunt of a bullfrog in the night.

Even in daylight the place made me uneasy. I slammed the car door harder than was necessary and tramped up the cracked stone steps. Here and there, green sprouted through the untended cracks. Wolfbane, I thought. The terrace had obviously been somebody's pride and joy years ago. Beautifully laid out, even neglect and decay could not obscure the artist's intention. I stood and looked along it admiringly, noting with disapproval the way the stonework had been left untended.

The man I had come to see was Reuben Adler, and he should have just enough loose change to keep his house in better repair. The Adlers had been with one of the first wagon trains that made it through the desert to the coast. They had unloaded their boxes, their pots and pans, old Mrs. Adler's battered piano, and set to work. Months of misery, hardship and danger behind them, they got right down to the job of building a new life. And build they did. Farmers at first, they quickly saw the possibilities of freighting, both by land and sea. When others rushed off to the goldfields in one bonanza after another, the Adlers stayed put. They farmed and freighted and raised huge families, who continued with the farms and the freight lines and also branched out into other enterprises.

By the turn of the century the Adler family were one of the greatest on the coast. What started the rot was the first war over in Europe. A number of the young men, on whom the future of the family depended, enlisted for France. They never made it, because three days out from New England the trooper ran into a pack of U-boats, and went down with all hands. That seemed to mark the turning point. The loss of their young men took some of the heart out of the elders, and the driving force was no longer there. The family began to split up, and gradually the empire crumbled. Not financially, but the power was no longer there, the control of the big corporations and business complexes. Now there was only one male Adler, the man I was visiting, Reuben. He must be in his late fifties, as near as I could judge. There had been a time when he had dreams of restarting the Adler myth. The first requirement was a number of sons, and

23

that was where he was beaten. By one of those inexplicable turns of fortune, Reuben could not sire a son. He married no less than four different women before he realised the fault lay in himself. Daughters presented no problem. If my memory served, there were five Adler girls, probably all married by now.

On the way out in the car I'd been searching in my memory for odd scraps of information about the family. As near as I could recall, the girls hadn't led a very happy existence with their father. His interest in them was boundless every time until they were actually born. Then, once he had heard the doctor's announcement, he took no further notice. They were not illtreated, they certainly never lacked for material comforts, but they might as well have had no father. And now, he lived here, more or less a hermit, in the great house built by his grandfather, old Josiah, last of the king-sized Adlers.

I stepped inside the huge porch and banged on the door. Almost at once, it was opened by an elderly woman in a plain black dress.

'Mr. Adler is expecting me,' I told her.

'This way, Mr. Preston.'

I don't know why I was surprised. According to all reports, the old man didn't have anybody to see him more than once in a blue moon. Naturally they would know who was coming.

The inside of the house was brighter, more cheerful than the exterior suggested. No draughty corridors for evil hunchbacks to scuttle down. The room she led me to was large, with a high domed ceiling. Furniture was heavy and expensive but not in a glaring modern way. People lived in this house, or had.

'I will advise Mr. Adler of your arrival.'

I wondered about the elderly woman, and where she fitted in. If she'd been twenty years younger I could probably have made a reasonable guess.

'I trust I have not kept you waiting, Mr. Preston.'

And he was there coming silently through a side door. He was slightly stooped, with coarse black hair now almost all white. His face was deeply lined, and carried within it a hint of remoteness. The clothes were rather a surprise. There was none of the velvet smoking jacket about Reuben Adler. He wore a well-cut and expensive suit of gray flannel. Despite the heat of the day the jacket was buttoned, and he wore a dark tie.

'It was good of you to come. Please sit down.'

He indicated a leather chair close by an old-fashioned leather-topped desk. When I sat, he nodded as though the arrangement met with his approval. Then he took another chair behind the desk, similar to mine except that his had arm-rests.

'You don't approve of my house,' he stated.

'Huh?'

It wasn't very polite, but the question took me by surprise.

'I saw you arrive,' he explained. 'I saw the way you took everything in. I also saw the expression on your face, Mr. Preston. It was disapproval.'

I shuffled my feet.

'Well — er — ,' I floundered. 'Er — not

at all, sir. It just seemed a pity, that is to say — '

His eyes twinkled.

'It just seemed a pity that such a splendid old house should not be properly maintained. Am I right?'

'It isn't any of my business, Mr. Adler.'

I felt like a fool, and must have sounded it.

'That is true,' he reproved. 'Nevertheless, since we are about to have a mutual interest, I shall explain to you. Do you know what this place is worth?'

'No. But I'd guess at eighty or ninety thousand,' I hazarded.

'Not bad. A little more than a hundred thousand in fact. For one elderly man to live in, that is somewhat extravagant, wouldn't you say?'

'Not if it's his own property,' I argued. 'A man has a right to his own.'

The bushy eyebrows waggled up and down.

'True. But there is a limit. At least, I choose to think so. But there is no one to whom I can pass this on. I have no heirs, you see. Once I am dead, the house will be sold. And with things the way they are, with property values reaching such ridiculous proportions, the value of this place does not lie in the house itself. It will be demolished, I've no doubt, and the entire estate split into housing lots. Do you think I'm wrong?'

'No, I don't suppose you are,' I admitted. 'But you said you haven't any heirs. Don't I recall you have a daughter, or even daughters?'

He pulled back his shoulders and looked at me fiercely.

'You do. I have daughters, five in fact. But they are married to men of some wealth. All except one that is. None of them is in need of this house and no one of them shall have it. It will be sold off, and the proceeds diverted to my estate.'

I nodded, and wondered about the fifth daughter.

'I don't quite see yet what business of mine any of this is, sir?' I confessed.

'None, Mr. Preston,' he said candidly. 'None whatever. I simply wanted you to see that it would be indefensible for me to spend large sums annually, for the purpose of keeping this place as it was in my grandfather's day. One man has no right to pamper himself that way.'

The latch clicked, and the woman who had opened the front door came in backwards carrying a silver tray.

'Ah, tea,' said Adler brightly. 'I always have a cup at four-fifteen. You will join me, Mr. Preston?'

'No, thanks,' I declined. 'A little hot for tea.'

'I can see you're no tea-drinker,' he reproved. 'Cooling and refreshing even on a hot day. What is it, Emily?'

The woman was standing with her hands clasped.

'Excuse me, sir, but cook is asking whether there will be company for dinner.'

Adler laughed lightly.

'You're nothing but a pack of nosey old women. I don't have many visitors, Mr. Preston. You've got them all excited. No, Emily, I don't think my business with Mr. Preston will take that long. And I'm certainly not telling either you or cook what he's come about.'

She sniffed and bustled out.

'You mustn't mind Emily,' he told me. 'These women here, they tend to be a little bossy at times.'

'All the staff are women?' I queried.

'Oh, yes.'

He said it matter-of-factly, but I gathered the question was unwelcome and I wasn't to pursue the subject.

'It's an odd sort of life I lead,' he went on. 'Unreal in some ways. Living alone, no family to speak of, no business interests A great deal of money, and nothing much to do with it. One could easily look inwards and finally die away.'

'Your appearance and your manner don't give that impression, if you'll forgive my saying so.'

'Thank you,' he was evidently pleased. 'I believe I have a worthwhile interest.'

A question was expected. I provided it.

'Really? May I ask what that is?'

'I am a numismatist, Mr. Preston. Do you know what that means?'

'No,' I confessed. 'I don't keep up with all the new religions.'

He smiled briefly.

30

'Numismatics,' he informed me, 'is not a religion. Although, even as I say that, I wonder whether indeed it would not be so considered by certain people of my acquaintance in the field.'

'Now you lost me,' I told him.

'Forgive me. A small joke. Numismatics is the science and study of coins and medals.'

It rang a bell now. Like most kids at some time or other I had gathered a small handful of worthless copper and silver coins years ago. Some were round, and some had funny shapes. A few had holes through the centre. I used to keep them locked in a special tin box, take them out now and again and study them with great care. They had odd words from many languages stamped on, and it used to be a secret annoyance that I couldn't even identify the country of origin half the time. My oldest coin was an English halfpenny dated 1904 and this I regarded as a rare object. It was my belief that if I kept the coins locked away, and the world knew nothing of them, they would gradually acquire great rarity and value.

Then I would triumphantly produce them and make a fortune. I might still have that dream, but I needed money for a new bicycle one time, and decided to make the sacrifice. I took the whole collection, about two dozen coins, to a dealer. He looked at each one with great care, checking against a printed reference book. Finally he offered seventeen cents for the lot.

Mr. Adler seemed to expect some comment, so I said,

'I see what you mean about religion.'

'Good. Although you are not personally knowledgeable on the subject you are no doubt familiar with the kind of grip an activity of this kind can take on a man?'

'Indeed yes. I also know the kind of money that's involved where big collectors are concerned.'

Stamps, coins, paintings. Take any physical and material shape that is associated with humanity and somebody somewhere is going to start collecting. A mystique builds up. Soon there are recognized authorities in the field, clubs and associations are formed. After a time somebody writes a text book, then a second one appears contradicting a lot of the theories in the first. Professional dealers get in on the act, then there are catalogues and works of reference. A whole private world is formed, and when you have a private world, you have to have orders of merit of some kind. These are of two kinds for the most part. Experts and big collectors. Sometimes the two things go together, but this is by no means automatic. Anybody with the necessary brains and application can become an expert. To be a big collector takes money, real money and lots of it. It is also true to say that all it takes to be a big collector is lots of money, and some of those who have it don't have the necessary brains to be experts. Judging by the house I was in, Adler could be a big collector. I wouldn't know whether he was an expert.

'You are a collector then, Mr. Adler?'

Again the brief smile.

'That is a fair description. Fortunately, I do not have a particular ego about it or I might almost be offended. However, for your information, I have one of the largest collections in the United States. Although I haven't exact details I believe there are two others in this country whose collections are larger than mine. That would not necessarily mean more valuable, of course.'

He was going well until he put in those last words. There were two bigger collectors so that made him third. But their collections were not necessarily more valuable because larger. He couldn't resist putting in that qualification, and that was the collector showing through. I was free to infer that his might be the most valuable in the country. Unfortunately for his intention, although I don't know anything about coins, I do know a little something about facts, and they don't just apply in one direction. If Adler's coins were not necessarily less in value than the larger collections, then by the same argument they were not necessarily more in value than some of the smaller. I'd come across collectors of other kinds before, and their little conceits were not quite foreign.

'I see,' I looked suitably impressed.

'And the reason you wanted to see me has something to do with the collection?'

I thought a direct finger like that might bring him quickly to the point. That just shows how much I really know about collectors.

'In a way,' he said evasively. 'First, I should like to tell you what kind of collector I am.'

He leaned back comfortably, and pressed the tips of his fingers together. I was about to get the lecture, and I felt the same quick desperation I sometimes feel when I find myself trapped at some meeting I don't want to attend. When that happens I'm usually in the front three rows and the exit is too far away for a fast fade. I half-expected the lights to dim so we could all see the slides better.

'To begin with,' he stated pompously, 'let us eliminate the lunatic fringe. There are such people, regrettably, far too many in my opinion. They are often people with nothing to occupy their time, who are looking for some respectable hobby — '

His voice almost shuddered as he used the word.

35

' — and who have sufficient means to indulge their fancy. They buy large quantities of coins, even perhaps medals on occasion, and of course they are not to be taken with any seriousness whatever. No, I am not including people of that kind at all when I speak of collectors. I refer only to serious collectors. Many of these are not men of wealth at all. They are people with a genuine regard for the subject, and a thirst for the knowledge it brings. Why, I know one such man for instance, who is a shoe store clerk, believe it or not. A most knowledgeable man, and one whom it is a pleasure to speak with. Yet, I doubt whether his personal collection is greater than a few dozen coins. You take my point?'

I nodded unhappily. I was trying to classify a certain nine-year-old boy I could remember. He had just a few dozen coins too, but I suspected that in Adler's book the boy would have been consigned to the lunatic fringe.

'Very well, we are speaking only of real collectors. These fall into two main categories, those who are interested in the romance of coinage, and those concerned only with the identification and classification of a given coin.'

'Whoa, Mr. Adler,' I held up a hand. 'This is a mite too fast for me. Could you break that last part down just a little more?'

He made an attempt, not too successful, to conceal his natural impatience with moronic private investigators.

'Certainly. You have to appreciate that the use of coins has been in existence a very long time. Have you any idea just how long?'

I hadn't any idea just how long. To keep from falling asleep I said,

'A thousand years?'

Adler smiled patronisingly.

'Let me just say this. It was a small cult among gentlemen of the Roman Empire to collect antique coins. Certainly there were coins in wide general use in the days of the Ancient Greeks. However, I don't want to get started on my subject, or we shall still be sitting here tomorrow morning.'

He laughed at his joke. I tried to

respond, but it sounded hollow. It seemed to me there was every possibility we should still be there the next morning.

'No, I must be as brief as possible. The point I am anxious to make is that coins of all sizes and values have been in use over a large part of the world for thousands of years. Their numbers are astronomical, and it takes a man of high intelligence many many years of study before he can begin to claim a real knowledge. Their approach is purely scientific, as indeed it has to be. They are concerned to examine a coin for evidence, evidence often of a kind which you as a detective would appreciate. When they have had twenty years of this kind of experience, they might be good enough to be recognised by others in the field as persons whose opinions are of value. Having said all that, I think you will agree that such a man has not the time, even if he had the inclination, to delve into the coins themselves.'

I was out in left field again.

'But I thought you said that was what he did do?' I objected.

'No. No, by no means. I said, or I intended to convey that the man employing this technical approach, that is to say identifying and classifying, tends to confine his interest to that and no more. In other words once he has satisfied himself, he will pronounce that the coin is such and such, and was probably struck round about such and such a date. His interest then ends. He cannot in all probability go on to tell you how the coin came into being, what political and economic influences were at work in the period and so forth. That is the province of the other kind of collector.'

The very self-satisfaction of his tone told me that Adler was to be included in the second category.

'They speak a language of their own, Mr. Preston. Every coin has a story to tell. A study of coins is a study of the human condition, and the development of mankind.'

He paused here, and it would have been the right moment for applause. I said,

'It must be very interesting, Mr. Adler.

I don't quite see yet — '

'I'm coming to it,' he cut in. 'All this is by way of a preliminary, in order that you can more readily grasp the story I am going to tell you.'

I nodded again, crushed at last. If all that had gone before had been by way of openers, I was going to regret not bringing a toothbrush by the time the main bout was concluded. Adler, on the contrary, was just warming up. He was getting into his stride with evident enthusiasm. Opening a drawer he took something out and laid it in front of me. It was a dull coin, not perfectly round and quite large.

'I am not going to ask you to guess what that is, Mr. Preston. I will tell you. It is a gold noble. You see the king in the ship?'

I peered at the worn lines and could almost make out a man holding a sword in one hand, something else in the other. The lower part of his body was cut off by a semi-circular line which was part of a ship if Adler said so. There were words faintly discernible around the perimeter, but I couldn't make them out.

'A Noble,' repeated Adler. 'Struck in the fifteenth century. The king is Henry the Fifth.'

Despite myself I was interested. Maybe it was Adler's enthusiasm communicating itself, or maybe there is in all of us that submerged interest in things long past. I picked up the coin and turned it over. On the other side there was some kind of cross in the middle, more words round the outside which I couldn't read.

'Five hundred years,' I muttered.

It seemed to please him.

'All that, and more,' he confirmed. 'Now look at this.'

He placed a second coin beside the first. It was the same dull colour.

'A bezant,' intoned my instructor. 'The gold coin of the Byzantine Empire. Unfortunately I am not one of the scientific people I was talking about, so I can't be absolutely certain of its age. Except of course, that it can't be more recent than 1453.'

'Why?'

'Because,' he explained patiently, 'that

41

was the year the empire finally collapsed, with the fall of Constantinople. As I say, I am not sufficiently well versed to speak with authority, but I would guess from the knowledge I have, that piece was struck in the thirteenth or fourteenth century.'

Utterly at his mercy now, I waited for the next revelation from the magician's bag.

'There is one more for you to see, and then I shall tell you a history. You will be more familiar with the name of this piece, if not its appearance.'

He was right on the second point at least. Its appearance meant nothing to me whatever. Adler smiled.

'A doubloon, Mr. Preston. The cause of all the trouble in those old pirate movies. The Spanish Main, the Caribbean, Henry Morgan. There isn't a limit to what the imagination can do with a doubloon. And that is the right period, too. In fact the doubloon was struck for hundreds of years, but to the average man it always means the sixteenth and seventeenth centuries.'

The average man had a look at the rather uninteresting coin, with its none-too-original portrait of a man's head. It seemed hardly to justify its reputation, but then, there's nothing very exciting about the appearance of an up-to-date U.S. currency bill, and I've seen people get very excited about those.

'O.K., Mr. Adler. Thanks for the lesson, and I have to admit it's all interesting. These coins,' I tapped at them. 'They seem to have originated in three very different places and times. What is the connection?'

'It's flattering to tell from your question that you have been paying more than passing attention,' he said in a pleased tone. 'As to the connection, Mr. Preston, I hardly dare dream of it.'

He looked around nervously at the closed doors and windows, as if expecting a call from Long John Silver.

'Have you ever heard of Seldon's Gold?' he demanded.

I thought quickly about the various names I'd heard associated with gold at different times. No Seldon.

'No, sir, I haven't.'

'One of the most romantic stories in the world of numismatics,' he assured me. 'And when I say that, Mr. Preston, I am saying a great deal, believe me. Perhaps some day, when we are not engaged on such pressing matters, you might like to visit me in a non-professional capacity. Then I could tell you some of those wonderful histories.'

I tried to look as though the idea appealed to me. In fact, it almost did, but if Adler's way of handling this interview was his idea of dealing with pressing matters, I shuddered to think how he would be when we had plenty of time.

'That may be a possibility, Mr. Adler. You were saying about Seldon's Gold —?'

'The name Seldon refers to one John Seldon, a gentleman attendant to the court of King Henry the Fifth of England. Some reference books, you will find, refer to him as Sir John or even Lord Seldon, but these are wrong. There was no title in the family in the early fifteenth century. Please smoke if you wish.'

My hand had made its umpteenth

involuntary search in my side pocket, and he'd guessed the reason. Nodding my thanks, I tapped out an Old Favorite and lit it. Adler refused.

'The king needed money and supplies for his war with France. He sent out several people with a carte-blanche to gather funds for the purpose. One of these entrusted with the work was John Seldon. Of course, in those days, it was not safe for a man of position to travel very far alone, certainly even more so with saddle-bags full of money. So Seldon had a party with him of five or six men, the exact number is not certain. They rode hard, for time was important, and they met with a good reception in most of the places they visited. They planned very sensibly, riding to the farthest point before making the first collection. In this way, you see, they would be homeward bound as the bags became heavier. The last call they made, or I should say, the last one on record, was to a place called Alden Hall, a few miles from the old town of St. Albans, and a comfortable ride from London. Here they were greeted with great hospitality, and the Baron swelled the bags with a personal donation of two hundred nobles, a very large sum. It so happens that the housekeeping accounts of the house have been preserved by the family, and so it is possible to verify the exact amount and the date and, by written evidence. The Baron estimated that the total sum carried by Seldon's men, when they rode out from the Hall, was not less than sixteen hundred nobles. Do I hold your interest, Mr. Preston?'

'You do. I'm all ears,' I admitted.

'Good. There was one more call due to be made by the collectors on their ride into London. Here the story is not so precise, because it is not known whether or not the party ever arrived. By the time it was realised something had gone wrong the master of the house had gone to war, and every man with him. The womenfolk and the children had been sent elsewhere since they had no men to protect them. What is certain is that neither men nor money arrived in London. When the king realised Seldon was long past due, he sent out other parties to search in case they had been waylaid by thieves on the roads, but nothing was found, not a trace. John Seldon, although a man of no great attainments, was a loyal and brave subject, and the king would not at first believe he had been betrayed. But when this seemed the only solution, he put a price on Seldon's head, and on that of every man with him. There was a great hue and cry, because here was a golden opportunity to win favour with the king, and pocket a handsome sum of money at the same time.'

'People don't change a lot, do they?' I put in.

'Regrettably no. Stories began to arrive thick and fast, as you can imagine. We need not concern ourselves with the hundreds of fake alarms. Luckily, we can sit at a comfortable distance and merely examine the truth. A trail was established. Three men, one of them riding the black charger which was undoubtedly Seldon's, had skirted London to the east. They had crossed the river in a ferry and headed for the Channel coast. Here they hired a boat and sailed for France.'

'You say there were three of them?'

'Yes. This is a matter of account from a number of eyewitnesses at different stages of the journey.'

'So somebody didn't make it?'

'Precisely. Either three or four men of the original party had dropped out of sight completely. Some months afterwards, two bodies were discovered in a wood, ten miles from London. They were identified from their clothing and so forth. One of them was Seldon's personal servant, and the other was almost certainly Seldon himself. The other man or men never materialised.'

'They'd been murdered, I suppose?'

'No doubt of it. There was a Scottish dirk wedged in the ribs of one of the skeletons. You appreciate, Mr. Preston, that although I am telling you a consecutive story, it was in fact many years before all the bits and pieces of evidence were so neatly fitted together.'

'Sure, I realise that. Please go on.'

'Who then were the three men on horseback? One was called Simon, his other name if he had one is lost. One was Andrew Petts and the third was merely known as the Miller. The one likely to have given the orders was Andrew Petts. He was a yeoman farmer with some ground of his own, and by the standards of the period not a poor man. The Miller could possibly have been a tenant of Master Petts. The man Simon remains somewhat of an enigma. We know almost nothing of him. Petts is the one of whom we know the most. He was for example a great drunkard and a roisterer, not unusual for the farmers of that day. He was also very free with the ladies, a fact which did not make him too popular with his fellows, not with the ones who had pretty wives or daughters anyway. Petts had daughters of his own, and being a farseeing man, had set them up in a stylish way of life in London. He did not wish them to spend their lives tied to farming. He thought London would provide wider opportunities and he was right. One of them met and married a French merchant in a fair way of business, one Simon de Pleuvet, another

Simon you see, just to confuse every-thing.'

'It hasn't become confused yet,' I assured him.

'When the girl went to France, she insisted her sister should go also. It wasn't long before she too was married to a Frenchman. So you can see, Master Petts had little stomach for the war with France. The task of helping John Seldon make his collection for the king must have seemed an opportunity sent from heaven. So he decided to help himself, talked these other men into assisting him, and stole the money.'

'But the French would give him a tough time, surely?' I queried.

'By no means,' he contradicted. 'Petts headed for the wine country. Wars and so forth meant little to the people down there, not then anyway. But they under-stood gold well enough. At first, it seems to have been Petts' intention merely to settle and live the life of a gentleman. But he quickly decided this was dangerous, and it wouldn't do to rely too much on his gold to buy hospitality. Indeed, after the way the war went for France he probably proved himself very wise. So he moved on, with the Miller. Something had happened to Simon meantime, and we have no facts to help us there. The next two years are blank entirely, then a great bull of an Englishman and a friend turned up in Amalfi. They had money, it seems, money enough to buy a fine house and live in style. The noisy one called himself Sir Andrew de Petteville, and the other was simply Mr. Miller.

'De Petteville?' I queried. 'Sounds more like a Frenchman.'

Adler shook his head.

'By no means,' he contradicted. 'You are forgetting your history, Mr. Preston. The Normans had been entrenched in England for almost four hundred years. Names of French origin were common-place particularly among the aristocracy.'

I looked suitably shamefaced, and decided to watch what questions I asked.

'To continue,' he resumed. 'These two apparently made quite a splash in Amalfi for a time. Then events took an unexpected turn. They suddenly abandoned their way of life and announced they would found a monastery. By the way, I ought to say at once that this part of the story is fully chronicled. There is no room for doubt as to its authenticity.'

I inclined my head to show I was still listening.

'They moved away from the town, which was of course also an important seaport, and into a large castle a few miles down the coast. Regrettably, the talk of a monastery proved to be rather misleading. The castle commanded a small but deep bay. It turned out that our two heroes had decided to take up piracy, and the bay was exactly what they needed for privacy and protection. In the next few years the Mediterranean and parts of the Adriatic were subjected to almost a reign of terror. So much so that the authorities, whom I may say were rather slack in such matters, finally decided they must do something about the nest of pirates de Petteville had recruited. They sent two companies of foot soldiers and one hundred good citizens to attack the castle.'

'That sounds like a quotation,' I suggested.

The old man beamed.

'Almost verbatim,' he confirmed. 'It's from Damietta's *Under No Flag*, probably the most authoritative reference work in existence on piracy. You recognised it?'

There he was again, hammering at my illiteracy.

'No, sir,' I hedged. 'Not exactly. Just the form of words you used.'

'Ah.' The tone said he hadn't expected much better. 'Well, of course they weren't going to catch the pirates unprepared. There was quite a battle on those cliffs. De Petteville, Miller and a dozen others deserted their fellows and sailed off with all their treasure. By this time of course, it was quite considerable. They knew they would not be safe again in Italy, and decided to make a complete breakaway. They went to the island we now call Crete, and started all over again. That part of the

53

Mediterranean is honeycombed with islands as you know. There were many rich trade routes to be plundered and de Petteville's cut-throats missed few opportunities. At last, the shipping lanes became so terrorised that a number of wealthy merchants of Athens actually commissioned their own fleet to attack the pirates on their own ground. The Battle of Olive Bay is of course history. The pirates were completely routed. The settlement was sacked, all their ships burned, and all but a very few were put to the sword.'

'De Petteville and the Miller,' I asked. 'Did they escape?'

'Not this time, Mr. Preston. They were executed with almost a hundred of their brethren.'

That sounded almost like the end of the picture, but there was no sign of the old boy bringing on the credit titles.

'So the treasure wound up in Greece?' I suggested brightly.

'Alas, no. The fleet sent by the merchants consisted of mercenaries and freebooters, many of whom were not above a little piracy themselves. One of these was a giant of a man named Vicente. Some authorities claim that he was a Spaniard of noble birth, but the plain fact is that although he was undoubtedly Spanish, he was no more than a common ruffian. This man and his crew located the greater part of de Petteville's hoard and made off with it while the rest of the fleet were busy setting fire to the town and roistering. Vicente knew he was dealing with people who'd spend their lives finding him if they had to. So he made the voyage all the way back to Spain. There he abandoned the sea for ever. He went far inland, to Madrid, and set himself up as a gentleman. So far as we know, he lived to an advanced age, a man of great wealth, and much respected. Now our story comes nearer the present time.'

Fool that I was, I believed him. I even leaned forward slightly.

'Yes,' his eyes gleamed. 'Almost two hundred years passed, and the Vicentes were now of course one of the most prominent families in the country. Then through some stupidity, some thoughtless act on the part of one of them, the Vicentes fell foul of the Inquisition. I need hardly expand on that, I think?'

For the first time I could not merely look intelligent, but feel it as well.

'I know how they worked,' I admitted. 'Torture, imprisonment, confiscation of property — '

Even as I said it, I realised the implications. Alder positively exuded pleasure.

'Yes, yes, I see you have it. You have it exactly. Seldon's Gold, Mr. Preston, swollen and multiplied by de Petteville and his cut-throats. Added to by two centuries of settled wealth by the Vicentes. A vast hoard, oh, one can only guess at its value in present-day terms. And now impounded by the Spanish authorities. From that point on its progress has been faithfully logged and recorded. No theories now, no guesswork. Entries in official registers, references in official dispatches, every one absolutely authenticated.'

'What happened then, sir?'

His eyes twinkled.

'It was a curious coincidence, though if you knew the way the inquisitors worked, you might think it something less than curious, that the King was in need of more funds for the conquest of Mexico. His armies were numerous, the expenses high. The Vicentes were given an alternative. One of the younger sons, Carlos, had already served as an officer in the army. He was to raise fifty men, arm and equip them himself. He would provide his own ship and crew. Then he would sail to the New World with the family fortune, plus certain other funds the King would entrust to his care.'

'In return for what?'

'The family would retain their lands, though not of course the fortune. And the family honour would be restored.'

Big deal, I thought privately. Out loud I said,

'Did he go for it?'

Alder was shocked.

'Go for it? I don't think you quite appreciate what I'm saying. We are speaking of a Spanish gentleman of the seventeenth century, sir. Honour was everything, absolutely everything. Money, land, even life itself, these things were nothing. But honour. I may tell you the King's offer was generous in the extreme. In the extreme. No gentleman of Vicente's standing would give the matter a second thought. Of course he grasped the opportunity with both hands.'

'What was to stop him outfitting the ship, and then disappearing with the take?' I asked innocently.

To tell you the truth, I was wondering how long it would be before we really got up to date. Say to about the year eighteen something. He frowned.

'I am sure that was a joke, although a poor one. Vicente would of course play his part as a gentleman. To resume, the ship sailed for Mexico. The voyage was long and perilous, but eventually she reached her destination. There can be no question of that. The landing took place on the eighteenth of November, 1641, at the place we now call Tampico. The epic journey that followed has been the subject of many fine books. I may mention one in particular, *Vicente's 500 Leagues*.'

I smiled politely.

'When Vicente arrived at Tampico he thought his mission was done. Unfortunately for him, he had been very sparsely informed before he left Spain. The eastern coastline was comparatively settled. The garrison for whom the funds were needed was at Mazatlan on the west coast. I think you will have some idea of what that meant.'

I thought about it briefly.

'I imagine it would mean around five hundred miles travelling,' I suggested.

He nodded obviously pleased.

'Quite. Quite. And across some of the hardest terrain in the world. Mountain, forests, wild beasts, not to mention the savage Indian tribes. And yet, despite sickness, poor food and Indian attacks, Vicente made that little trip, sir, in four months. I really must lend you the book.'

'Just a moment,' I objected. 'I thought you said the book mentioned leagues. Stop me if I'm wrong, but a league used to be three miles. Five hundred would be fifteen hundred miles.'

I never did learn when to keep quiet. Adler bounced with pleasure.

'Absolutely correct. Absolutely. At the end of this fantastic undertaking, Vicente learned that he was to join an expedition to the north.'

He passed a hand over his face, as though suddenly tired.

'I really mustn't carry on this way, or I shall be telling you about every camp fire they lit.'

The same point had occurred to me.

'Well, sir, I'll be brief. The expedition was treading little new ground. There had been several to the north during the preceding thirty years or so. But this one was not altogether military in its purpose. It was to travel to what the commander considered the limit of human endurance. At that point a town would be built. So there were women and children, cattle and household goods. In the event, after almost a year, this huge caravan, mostly on foot, reached their limit. They founded their town five hundred miles to the north of Mazatlan. A great part of Vicente's treasure was still with them, though of course it was now government money. At first, all went well. But before long, some of the men began to fret. They were adventurers, soldiers, it was no part of their scheme of things to till the land and build houses. Early in 1645, a band of these men broke into the treasury during the night. They killed the guards, and made off with the gold and most of the best horses. Vicente was a prominent man in the town, naturally. He took it as a personal affront, although the money was no longer his. He recruited a small force of ten men, and set off once again. It seemed little more than a simple policing job on the surface. In a few days he would catch the thieves and return. But they had planned well in advance. They had the better horses, and of course had taken extra ones with them in anticipation of pursuit. They bribed Indian tribes to harass their pursuers. The chase lasted for almost a month, then Vicente caught up with them. There was a fight and several on both sides were killed. The thieves surrendered, and they started homewards. Now this is most important. At the time they were caught, they had reached a point which has been argued hotly for many years. But there is general agreement on one thing. They had almost certainly reached a spot somewhere between San Diego and Yuma.'

'That narrows it down,' I said, trying not to sound too caustic. 'That must be about a hundred and fifty miles. Give 'em guessing space of twenty miles north or south and you have, let's see, around six thousand square miles.'

He bobbed his head.

'That is almost exactly correct, Mr. Preston. And now I will tell you why that is important. The party was suddenly attacked by Indians, and massacred. Only one man escaped. Months later, he reached a Spanish settlement and told his story. Because of the treasure, search parties were sent out. They were only the first of many. Over the years, many attempts have been made to locate the site of the Vicente massacre, all without success. Indeed, I may tell you that twenty years ago, I myself took part in one of these.

All we got were callouses on our hands.'

I looked at the three coins on the table. Whether it was the story itself, or merely Adler's enthusiasm communicating, I don't know. But I felt a sensation, a kind of tingle as I stared at those round pieces of metal. Almost unconsciously, my hand reached out to touch them. He watched with approving eyes.

'That's a very good story, Mr. Adler,' I said softly. 'A beautiful story. We seem to be getting near something like a happy ending, I gather?'

He breathed emotionally.

'Ah,' he replied wistfully. 'If only one could be convinced of that. But I may say, yes, I think I may say, one dares to hope.'

I broke out the Old Favorites and pushed one into my face.

This was what I'd come to hear.

2

Adler held his hands together in front of his face as if he were praying. Slowly he tapped the four fingers of one hand against the four fingers of the other.

'Three weeks ago,' he intoned, 'I had a telephone call from a man who asked whether I would be interested in buying some old coins. He didn't sound like a man one would normally find in that line of business. Nevertheless, I agreed to see him.'

'Here?' I interjected.

'No. And that struck me as odd. He wouldn't come to the house. He said I was to meet him in the city. I refused, thinking it might be some underhand affair. One is sometimes offered stolen property, you see?'

'Yes. So you wouldn't go?'

'No. Then he said he'd send a sample which would change my mind. Next morning in the mail I received this.'

He picked up the noble and fondled it.

'There was no note, nothing with it at all. Of course I was enormously interested at once. I fretted for hours because I hadn't taken the simple precaution of asking the man for a telephone number. That afternoon he called again. I asked him many questions, but he wouldn't answer one. He wouldn't even tell me his name. I said to him — ' and Adler chuckled at the wicked thought — 'suppose I keep the noble and refuse to pay for it. Of course, it was nonsense, I could never do such a thing. Do you know what he said?'

'Uh, uh.'

The collector wrinkled his forehead trying to recall the exact words.

'He said, 'Mr. Adler, this is not a ten-cent deal. You want to keep it, keep it. This is a real big deal, Mr. Adler. We got dozens like that.''

I jumped in quickly.

'You're quite certain he said 'we'?'

'Oh, yes. Absolutely. It wasn't the only time he used the plural.'

So already there was a 'we'. That meant

two or more, and that meant some kind of operation.

'Then he suggested another meeting,' I muttered.

'Yes. For that same evening. I was to meet someone at the Piute Hotel. That's down in an undesirable section near the outskirts of the fruit country.'

I stared at him. If anybody else had said that to me I'd have known it was a rib. But Adler was completely poker-faced. I guess a man who lives practically alone in a big house in the big money belt doesn't have a lot of experience of places like the Piute. There was probably some joint in Monkton with a worse reputation, but off-hand I couldn't recall it. At the Piute, everything went. It was a tequila joint with gambling in some of the upstairs rooms and what you'd expect in the others. It was dirty, one step up from a flophouse, and the clientele was almost hand-picked by the proprietor. To get in you had to be unwashed, unshaven, and preferably with a police record.

'Did you actually go there?'

'You sound surprised. Certainly I went.

I was intrigued far more than I can tell you. Mind you I was a little — er — surprised at the surroundings, but they counted for little.'

Little is right. I reflected. With the Piute customers the surroundings count for precisely nothing at all.

'This man you spoke to,' I queried, 'he still hadn't given you a name?'

'No. But that no longer mattered. I was only interested in this little beauty and the talk about dozens of others. Well, I got into the place, and went up to the bar, the way the man had instructed. I asked the bartender for champagne, also on instructions. Then I had another surprise. The bartender said I was to give him five dollars for his trouble. I was in no mood to quibble about five dollars. I gave it to him, and he said something about me being the right guy. Then he handed me an envelope. Inside was the doubloon. Again, no message, nothing. I asked to see the man who'd left the envelope, but the bartender knew nothing about him. All he knew was, a man came and left that envelope for me to collect. And he was to tell me that would be all for that evening, and I'd receive a further telephone call next day.'

I looked for somewhere to park the butt. Adler slid across a silver ashtray mounted in cowhide. It seemed a pity to make it dirty.

'I was slightly put out to find that the man was not going to keep our rendezvous. But I must confess, I was also beginning to enjoy the game.'

'Had you any reason to doubt the authenticity of either of these coins?' I demanded. 'I mean no offence to your knowledge of the subject, Mr. Adler, but you are in fact expert enough to be certain both were genuine?'

He was not offended.

'I accept that question without rancour,' he said pompously. 'You think I could be just a rich man playing at a hobby without really knowing the subject. That was true once, up until about ten years ago. But my attitude is very different now. Very different indeed. I spend a great deal of time on the subject, as well as money. And I'm not a fool.'

I acknowledged this little rebuke with a faint grin.

'Oh, they were genuine enough,' he went on. 'Or I should say 'are'. The next day there was no telephone call. Nor the next day, nor the day after that. In fact, almost a week went by. I was beginning to get quite worried. After all, here I was in possession of two rare and quite valuable coins, neither of which was my property. But finally came another call. The man said he'd had to go out of town on some other business and hadn't been able to keep our appointment. He'd left the noble instead as a token of his good faith. Well, I was very relieved to hear from him again. I told him so, and we made another appointment.'

'For the Piute?' I asked.

'No. This time he wanted to see me at a place called the Meadowlark. It's some ten miles from the city, perhaps you know it?'

Perhaps I did. Big Joe Meadows' place was a far cry from the Piute. At the Piute the unwashed clientele got ill on tequila. At Big Joe's it was champagne and very old brandy, but very old. At the Piute you could have a whale of a time for fifty cents and a little walk upstairs for another four bits. Not so at the Meadowlark. There you needed at least fifty bucks for a few belts and a sandwich. There wasn't any upstairs, at least not that kind of upstairs. But a word with Salvatore, the captain of waiters, might just produce the name of a lady consultant, whose business it was to understand and minister to the needs of those who could pay the tab at the Meadowlark. And speaking of tabs, if you wanted Salvatore to put you in touch with such a lady, you would need to put Salvatore in touch with some of the local currency. The more I thought about it, the less of a far cry it seemed from the Meadowlark to the Piute Hotel.

'I know the place,' I confirmed. 'This would be when exactly?'

'Let me see, it was the week before last, on a Tuesday. He wanted to meet me the next night, Wednesday, at nine o'clock in the evening. I went, naturally. I also took with me these coins, because if nothing should come of our little discussion, why then they would of course have to be returned to their owner.'

'Assuming the guy who sent them to you had any right to them in the first place,' I qualified.

'Assuming that, yes. Remember, at this point, I still had no idea of the other man's identity. I was to wait in the club bar, and he would approach me. It was all unusual of course, but I didn't mind too much about that. To tell you the truth, Mr. Preston, I was enjoying the whole thing. I don't get out too much these days, and this little intrigue was quite a welcome diversion in my life.'

He needn't have told me that. His every inflection and gesture yelled aloud that Reuben Adler was enjoying himself one huge piece. To show I was paying attention, I said,

'And this time he showed?'

He nodded.

'Oh, yes. Why, I was hardly inside the place before he made himself known to me. He was a big man, not so exceptionally tall that is, but very very broad in the shoulders. In fact he looked like a fighter, you know? A heavy coarse sort of face, and his nose looked to have been damaged in an accident. Oh, yes, and he had two scars on his cheek. He wasn't the kind of man one would normally choose to do business with. In fact, if he'd approached me on the street on a dark night, I think I would have run away.'

He laughed at his little joke, and I forced a little joke look onto my face.

'What about his clothes?' I asked. 'They're a mite particular who they let through those hallowed portals out there.'

'That was the thing. That was just the thing. His clothes were every bit as good as my own, perhaps better. We got some drinks and sat down. Then he told me a very odd story. I won't bother you with it now, but he knew where there was this large box of coins. All like these. Of course, he didn't claim they were all the same, because as he freely admitted, once he got away from dollars and cents, he was lost.'

'Mr. Adler, I think I'd better hear the

story. Everything I've heard up to now screams of stolen property. And that kind of merchandise is no fit company for me.'

'Fair,' he murmured. 'Yes, I think that is fair. I'll leave out most of it, though you may ask questions if you wish. It seems there is a certain village in Baja California close by an old Aztec ruin. The ruin itself is not worthy of being preserved, since it is very crude, and very little of it remains. The Mexicans believe the place to be haunted by evil spirits, and they shun the place. A small boy went there, following a dare by his fellows, and in a small cave nearby, he found the box. He hadn't any idea of its value, naturally, but he seems to have been a very advanced boy. He told neither his parents nor the priest. Instead he went to the proprietor of the local — er — well, the equivalent of the Piute Hotel. This man saw at once there might be a chance of profit. He in turn went to those in the nearest city who would know more about such things. As a result my scar-faced friend got in touch with me.'

'Just like that?'

'Not quite as easily as that of course. The people who were approached in the city also knew nothing of coins and such, but they had the advantage of access to information. They could find out those who did know about such things. And so, eventually, they got into touch with me.'

'You didn't tell me the name of the man with the scars,' I reminded.

'At that point I did not know it myself. I have learned it since, but' — he sensed another question — 'please let me continue the tale in the same sequence in which it happened.'

'Sorry. Go on.'

'The man told me this story. For your benefit I have trimmed it down to essentials. But I questioned him very closely on many points. He was very frank with me, except when it came to the whereabouts of the box. I began to think, indeed I must admit it had crossed my mind before, that this man might be the link with Seldon's Gold. He said this was just a preliminary chat, and he wanted me to take at least a week to think about it. After that, if I was definitely interested, we could have another talk. If not, I wouldn't hear from him again. Oh, and he said something rather strange. He said if I decided against the proposal, there would be no hard feelings.'

It may have sounded strange to Adler, but to me it made a lot of sense. This was the tryout, the feeler. On a deal like that, when a man with a scarred face and an expensive suit says there won't be any hard feelings, that is very good news for whoever he's talking to. But I didn't burden Mr. Adler with these little insights into the criminal mind.

'That's nice,' I commented. 'So then he gave you the third coin.'

He looked faintly surprised.

'Why, yes he did. He said he'd been asked especially to be sure I got it, and that I kept all three while I was making up my mind.'

Naturally. You leave a collector with three choice pieces, tell him there's plenty more where they came from. You leave him to boil for one week, while he's making up his mind. But of course he isn't doing anything of the kind. He's spending that week staring at the pieces, fingering them, dreaming about them. He's just waiting for that week to end so he can set his hands on the rest.

'Very smart,' I admitted. 'Was anything said about money?'

'That was another odd thing,' he replied. 'I asked how much he was hoping for. He said he would be prepared to leave it up to my honesty how much I paid. He could not consider anything lower than one hundred thousand dollars, but the collection was worth far more. He would leave it for me to decide what was a fair price.'

'A hundred thousand sounds like a lot of price to me,' I told him.

Adler wagged his head vigorously from side to side.

'By no means, Mr. Preston, by no means. A great deal of money, to be sure, but not a fraction of the value of Seldon's Gold. Not a fraction. To say nothing of being the possessor of such a hoard. Why, in the world of numismatics, I would become almost a legend myself. Be assured, the money asked was most reasonable.'

Different people have different values. I know two or possibly three people who would think a hundred grand a very great deal of money.

'Mr. Adler, maybe I'm missing a point here. You said before you met the man you'd had a feeling this might turn out to be a lead to Seldon's Gold. You found his story enough corroboration to convince you?'

'Almost enough,' he confirmed. 'But a story, Mr. Preston, is only a story. If I got worked up about every story I hear, I'd be a nervous wreck. No, sir, the story alone, though powerful, did not convince me. This,' he tapped at the third coin, 'this, sir, was what did it. I see you don't quite follow me?'

'I'm trying,' I assured him.

'Then consider. First, a noble, then a doubloon. Both excellent coins, and a most interesting combination in themselves. One could weave a pretty fantasy around the circumstances which would bring two such coins together. But, and this is an important but, the occurrence is not without precedent. Those were days when there was much piracy in the Caribbean. For some pirate captain to have both nobles and doubloons in his chest would not have been such a rare thing. But this little beauty, the bezant, that put an entirely different complexion on the whole thing. This means the East, Mr. Preston. And for this to be found with the others, reduces the complex of theories drastically. In fact, sir, it reduces the possible rational explanations down to one. Seldon's Gold.'

His eyes glittered as he ran caressing fingers around the coins.

'Seldon's Gold it has to be. And I am on the verge of locating it.'

'I get it. And you want me to help out as an escort with the cash.'

'Cash?'

'They wanted the money in cash, didn't they? This doesn't sound to me like a credit operation.'

He held up a hand for silence. There was silence.

'They did insist on cash,' he admitted.

'But you are getting ahead of my story again.'

I mumbled something and stared at the ashtray.

'Remember I had one week to consider his proposal. The man said he would call me for my answer on the following Wednesday. If I wished to proceed we would arrange a further meeting. He called as promised, and I arranged to be at the Meadowlark again that night.'

'This would be Wednesday of last week?'

'Correct.'

'Were you to take the money with you?'

He chuckled.

'Really, Mr. Preston, you must take me for a fool. Of course I would never consider doing any such thing. No, the purpose of the meeting was to go into details as to how and where we should make our bargain.'

Now, finally, I could see where I fitted in. I was to go with him to talk to these guys. A man can get frustrated when he's wrong so often.

'Yes,' he continued. 'That was to have

been the last of our preliminary meetings. Unfortunately my friend did not arrive. I waited an hour, left a message at the bar, and came home. I was bitterly disappointed.'

He opened a drawer, took out a newspaper clipping and laid it flat on the desk.

'I didn't feel too disheartened about it, because there had been an earlier occasion when he had been unable to keep the appointment. I thought he would be calling again. The following afternoon I learned this was unlikely to happen.'

He slid the clipping across to me. There was a very bad picture of an obviously dead man. But even the worst picture couldn't hide the nose and those two long scarlines. I remembered all about it at once. The guy had been dumped in the sea in the middle of the night, and recovered almost immediately by a local deep-sea fisherman. It had all the ear-marks of a mob kill, and a couple of days later this was more or less confirmed when the body was identified. It was a man named Toots McKern, well-known to the police authorities in Yuma, Arizona.

'So your guy was McKern,' I mused.

'I see you followed the case.'

'That's how I stay in business, Mr. Adler. I have to keep in touch,' I pointed out gently. 'The late Mr. McKern was from Yuma, and that suggests something to me.'

'Precisely. It gives added weight to the whole thing. Yuma is no distance from the border, no distance at all. And it fits in with every scrap of evidence that's ever been gathered, that Yuma would be the furthest point east the treasure could have reached.'

I looked at Toots again, and decided he must have been a very ugly guy, even when his features were moving.

'So we seem to have arrived at a dead end, Mr. Adler. And I didn't intend that to be funny. What did the police say?'

'Police?'

'Well, you've presumably told them your story?'

He got up and paced around. I knew the answer would be in the negative, but I was wondering why he was taking so long about telling me. Just as suddenly he sat down again.

'Mr. Preston, I have not informed the authorities of this business.'

I tried to look surprised.

'Am I allowed to ask why?'

'There are two main reasons. There are smaller ones too, but I don't regard these as of real significance.'

'Let's hear the big ones,' I suggested.

'Well — ' he hesistated — 'I suppose I am correct in assuming you will not repeat a word of this outside this room?'

I smiled my open boyish smile.

'Mr. Adler, you may safely assume that anything you say to me which ought to be known to the police will be repeated word for word downtown within two hours.'

'Eh?' he looked startled. 'Oh, I see. A joke.'

'Mr. Adler,' I said patiently, 'I know my jokes are bad, but there is a decent limit. I mean every word I say. If you know anything about this murder, or have a lead to stolen property or the like, get another boy.'

He frowned with displeasure.

'But you're a private investigator. I had you looked up. People speak very highly of your services. I thought you could respect a confidence.'

'Sure.' I always have a tough time explaining my precarious position to people. 'I can respect a confidence. I also respect the boys downtown, and in their narrow-minded suspicious way they have some kind of respect for me too. Because, believe it or not, in my own unorthodox way, I'm on the same side they are, and they know it. No bones have been broken. We had a nice chat. If you want me to leave now, it's O.K. by me. There won't be any charge.'

'No, no, wait. I don't think I'm doing anything wrong. Let me explain to you, and you can decide whether you wish to help or not.'

I settled back on the chair I'd been about to vacate.

'Two main reasons, you said,' I prompted.

'Very well. The first one is by far the most important. The man McKern was not alone in this. There are others involved. I am not the only man in the country who is both wealthy enough and interested enough to buy this hoard. If I go to the police, they will certainly have nothing further to do with me. They will take their business elsewhere. It would amount to no more than simple prudence on their part.'

Which was true enough. And it was understandable to me that Adler would scarcely enthuse if it happened.

'And the other?'

'The other is that I do not yet have possession. The story would get into the newspapers and collectors, some far bigger than I, from all over the world would flock here. It would be like, what shall I say, a millionaires' convention.'

'And the boys could have a high old time auctioning to the highest bidder,' I commented.

'That would be one result. The other would be to start off a legal battle that might last for years. Consider the history of that gold. Think of what I've told you here today. We have a saying in this country that gold is where you find it, but that is not necessarily true of Seldon's Gold. It could be claimed by the governments of Mexico and possibly Spain. By the Vicente family, if indeed there are traceable descendants. By the family of the small boy who stumbled across it. Why man, it could grow into one of the most involved international legal tangles of the century.'

'I see your point. But surely, that could happen anyway? I mean suppose you get hold of it, that still wouldn't change the legal position.' He nodded wisely.

'In one material respect, yes. I would have it. I might become the disputed owner, but I would be the owner. And I think I would put up quite a fight to retain that status.'

I started thinking out loud.

'Sure. But if it all starts up before you get your hands on it, you don't have any status at all.'

'Exactly, exactly. Whatever came out of the arguments all the other people might raise, I would have no position in the case. I would simply be a man who happened to know about it.'

I stared at the gleaming silver interior of the ashtray again. The thing had a kind of fascination for me.

'Mr. Adler, I can see that from where you sit, there seems to be a good reason for not going to the police.'

'And from where you sit?'

I rubbed at my cheek. There wasn't anything the matter with it. It's one of those little time-wasters that keeps the action going while I'm trying to make up my mind what to say.

'All you know about McKern's murder is what you read in the papers?'

'Yes. It's an odd question.'

'Not so odd. Is there anything you left out of your story? Like for instance, has anybody else been in touch since McKern dropped out of the picture?'

'Not as yet. I've been expecting it naturally. Or perhaps I ought to say, hoping for it.'

I did the cheek bit again.

'Technically, you're in the wrong, Mr. Adler. Wait — ' as he was about to interrupt — 'I don't go in too much for technicalities. What you ought to do is go to the police and tell your tale. But you know nothing of the actual murder. Therefore you are not withholding evidence connected with it, not directly at least. And I do see the rest of it, and it sounds absolutely right to me.'

He sat there listening, evidently relieved at what I was saying.

'In your spot, Mr. Adler, I would hire somebody like me. Somebody very like me.'

He smiled.

'That was why I asked you here in the first place.'

I lit a fresh cigarette and looked at him through the smoke.

'Now you tell me what you have in mind.'

The fine hands fluttered.

'I've no idea at all. I want to get my hands on that box of money. I haven't the faintest notion of how to set about it. The position is that I am compelled to sit here, in the hope that sooner or later I will be contacted. I haven't any way of knowing whether that will ever happen. I feel I must be doing something, anything, but I don't know what. That's why I asked you to come. You are experienced in such matters.'

Oh, sure. I'm probably the greatest expert in the world. Hardly a day goes by but I don't dig up some old pirate's chest, or stumble across a lost city of the Incas. This assignment looked like a lulu.

'I'll think of something,' I promised. 'I guarantee nothing, and you'd better know that from the start. Also, I shall need some money. You'd be surprised what terrible memories people develop after a murder. I may have to spread a dollar bill here and there.'

He was already opening a flat wooden box he'd taken from the desk.

'Would a thousand dollars get you started?'

It would. So would five hundred, but I didn't bother Mr. Adler with that. I put the sheaf of bills in my billfold and got up.

'Only one thing I insist on,' I said. 'If these people get in touch with you, I must be told.'

'Agreed.'

'Have you ever told any of this to anybody else but me?'

'No. You will find that even the most loose-tongued collector can become extremely close-mouthed when he's on the track of something good.'

'Very well. I'll be in touch.'

We shook hands and I went out. Emily, the housekeeper, materialised from nowhere in time to open the front door. I bowed gravely, because Emily was the kind of old-fashioned lady who is entitled to a little grave bowing, and went down the cracked steps to the car.

My head was full of Spanish galleons and corsairs, the Tower of London, Aztecs and swamp fever, pirates' gold and all that Henry Morgan. It was lucky I hadn't worn my armour today. The sun was too hot.

3

One of the features of Monkton City that
the city fathers needn't be ashamed of is
the municipal library. This is not only a
fine and imposing structure, but it also
has one of the largest and best selections
in the entire state. I went into the cool
and found we had a new lady assistant
librarian. By tradition, lady librarians are
supposed to be severe, homespun, and
built to look like an extra bookshelf. This
gal was no respecter of tradition. She had
bubble-cut blonde hair and a cute nose
that turned up just enough. The thick
tortoiseshell glasses were supposed to
make her look studious, I imagine. All
they did was accent how attractive she
was.

'Can I help you?'

She was very formal. There was none of
that I'm a dish and I know what that look
on your face means. She was there to help
out with the book business, and I had

better get that straight from the start. I looked business-like too.

'Do you have any works of reference on numismatics, please?'

She looked startled.

'What subject did you say?'

'Numismatics,' I repeated. 'It's the study of coins.'

'I am aware of that, sir. I'll show you the shelf.'

I was puzzled as I followed the trim little figure between the rows. It was a library, wasn't it? They had books about coins, didn't they? They presumably had those books because they figured there was an outside chance somebody might like to look at one some day. So why the reaction from this one? Maybe I just didn't look like a guy who would want to know about old coins. That must be it.

'Here we are,' she whispered. 'I'm afraid we don't have very many. It's rather a specialised subject of course.'

'Of course,' I smiled. 'And thank you.'

She nodded formally to indicate the interview was ended and flounced away. When she was out of sight I got back to the books. Most of them looked too technical for me. I settled for a slim volume called *Discover the Wonders of Coins*. A quick flick at the pages showed this was the kind of stuff I was after. I took the book to a reading table and settled down to a quiet browse. I quickly found myself interested. The author had been aiming at people like me, looking for quick and easy knowledge without any grasp of the subject. My intention was to find out about nobles, doubloons and bezants. Some people might think that shows a lack of faith in my employer, but some people don't know some of the employers I've had.

There was nothing in the descriptions or the photographs that contradicted anything Adler had told me. The whole thing was fascinating and my eyes kept wandering off to other coins, other histories. Suddenly I realized I wasn't alone. There was a man standing beside me. When he didn't move, I looked up.

'Hi, Preston.'

Detective First Grade Schultz of Homicide grinned down at me.

‘Hallo, Schultzie. I didn’t know you were a bookworm.’

‘I practically live here,’ he assured me. ‘But I can’t stay now. I have to go.’

‘Don’t let me hold you back.’

I bent my head to the book again. He didn’t go away.

‘The idea is,’ he explained gently, ‘that you come with me. Cap’n wants to see you.’

‘Huh?’ My astonishment was not faked. ‘What about?’

‘Who knows? The Captain says to me, go get Preston down here, I go. I don’t even stop to ask him why. I just do it. Let’s go.’

It would be useless to argue. I sighed and got up.

‘You won’t mind if I put this back where it came from?’ I said sarcastically.

‘Be my guest. I always wanted to meet somebody who put a library book back in its proper place.’

I put the wonders of coinage back with its fellows, and we headed for the door. Bubble-cut bent her head as we went past. Maybe she thought Schultz might attack her. A thought struck me outside.

'Hey, when did Rourke ask for me?'

'Oh, 'bout ten minutes ago,' he replied. 'Take your own car, and I'll see you at headquarters.'

'Ten minutes ago,' I called as he walked away. 'Then how'd you know where to find me?'

He waved as he climbed in the police sedan. I got into the Chev and turned to follow him. I wondered what Rourke wanted. We didn't have any unfinished matters between us. And yet he must be in a hurry to send one of his squad out for me. Ah, well, at least I didn't have to worry about it. I hadn't put a finger out of place in weeks. Whatever Rourke wanted was all right with me. For once, Preston was clean.

I guess there are some of us who just don't ever learn.

Odd that I should visit two of our most important public buildings one after the other. As I said, the library is a town feature. So is the police building, but at the other end of the scale. It was built before World War I, and at the time it was one of the most impressive police headquarters in the state of California. The world has moved on a little in the last half-century or so, but the headquarters building remains as a monument to the past. Unfortunately, it was possible in those early days to run the town with a sheriff and about ten constables. They must have been mighty proud of their fine offices, and of all the spare room they had. Nowadays the same space had to fit the greater part of a hundred and fifty officers of all kinds, plus all their equipment. They felt slightly cramped at times. I've even heard harsh words against the administration, which leaves the guardians of the public safety squashed in such a hovel, but will cheerfully pay out millions on new prisons. The world goes ahead. The enemies of society have to be incarcerated, but there's no need for inhumanity. They must have adequate living space, air conditioning in summer, a good system of heating in winter. They must have it, and they get it. Naturally, this makes a hole in the public funds, and what more obvious than to save as much as possible on other civic expenditure? Such as the police building, for instance.

The Homicide Detail is on the third floor of this palace. You can take a chance in the creaking and temperamental elevator, or else trudge up the grooved and worn flights of stairs. Experienced people such as Detective Schultz and, regrettably myself, always choose the stairs. After the first few visits you don't any longer notice the stained and cracked walls, the dusty fly-blown light fittings and the general air of decay. The Detail is allotted exactly three rooms up there. The end one had a door half-panelled in glass. Not that it made any significant difference. The grime of years was encrusted into that glass, which was the mark of seniority of the occupant of the end office. The legend reads, 'Captain of Detectives — J. Rourke', and that's another sample of how tight they hold those purse-strings down at City Hall. Rourke held the office, but not the rank. He was a lieutenant only, the city not being able to afford the extra two thousand a year that went with a captain's badge.

Rourke shares the office with Gil Randall, his sergeant. Gil wasn't there today but Rourke was very much in evidence. He looked up sourly as we marched in.

'Preston, Lieutenant,' reported Schultz.

'Kay. Get back on that other thing now, huh?'

Schultz got out and closed the door.

'Siddown, siddown.'

The grizzled Irishman waved me to the battered wooden chair reserved for visitors. He was almost affable, but that didn't mean a thing.

'Smoke if you want.'

I wanted. He took from the desk one of those poisonous little black cheroots of his, and inspected it with approval. Then he flicked a match into life with his thumbnail and sent the first cloud of stinging yellow smoke billowing into the confined atmosphere. It has always been a contention of mine that those weeds of Rourke's are as good as an extra man on the squad. After a couple of hours' exposure to the fumes, plenty of people would be glad to sign anything.

'You haven't been getting in my hair lately, Mark. That's good, that's very good. I'd been sort of hoping you might make a habit of it.'

His brilliant eyes were fixed on me through the evil cloud. I puffed out smoke from my Old Favorite which was immediately engulfed and swallowed by the swirling fumes. You could practically hear the cheroot laugh.

'I don't like to get in people's hair, John,' I said carefully. 'Just try to make an honest dollar here and there.'

He sniffed.

'I haven't time to quarrel with that ridiculous statement right now. You know what I want. Let's have it.'

I felt quietly triumphant. For once Rourke was going to goof, and that didn't happen too often. I hadn't the faintest idea what he was talking about. Trying not to smirk, I said,

'You have me, John. How would I know what you want? You didn't ask me anything yet.'

'I see.'

He chewed at the butt in his mouth, rolling it from side to side, and never once taking his eyes off me.

'I'm disappointed,' he announced. 'You know, you being such an honest citizen and everything. Thought you might like to give a few pointers to a poor old public servant. You know, like give me a shove in the right direction.'

'Always glad to help the police,' I said cautiously. 'Which direction did you have in mind?'

He slammed his great fist down on the scarred wooden table.

'Don't come in here fooling around with me, Preston. I'm a busy man, and my temper isn't all it should be. You know what I want. What do you know about this Toots McKern killing?'

'Huh?'

My jaw must have dropped. I have great respect for Rourke and the way he works. I never underestimate him, nor Randall either. But this was from the fourth dimension. There was no way, but no way, he could possibly know I had any connection with McKern. Dammit, I hadn't known myself an hour before. Unless Adler — but no. That would be ridiculous.

'The guy you pulled out of the ocean? I'll tell you everything I know about him. Name Toots McKern. Occupation, hoodlum. Territory, Yuma, Arizona. Age 43. Cause of death, bullet wounds in back. That's all it said in the *Bugle*, and that makes it all I know. I never laid eyes on the man, before or after you got him.'

He drummed on the table with thick fingers, trying to control mounting irritation. It was a good sign. It indicated he hadn't really got anything to tie me to McKern, and had just been hoping to surprise something out of me. Because when Rourke has something, he seldom gets irritable. He plays from a good hand, and just waits for the opposition to fold.

'Guy like you must have a lot of interests,' he said surprisingly. 'Getting around all the bars, and most of the dames. An intellectual kind of existence.'

'It suits me,' I told him. 'And don't believe all the things you hear. Mostly my life is pretty dull.'

He nodded.

'Sure, I know. You got any hobbies?'

'Huh?'

'You know, like some guys fool around with carpentry or do a little metal work. Some collect things, like stamps for instance.'

'Uh, uh,' I negatived. 'I never got around to any of those things.'

He smiled, and it was not pleasant.

'How about the coin racket? What do they call it, numismatics? How 'bout that?'

I went very still inside, but I knew better than to take my time about answering. That way, he would know I was watching my tongue.

'I don't know the first thing about it,' I replied easily.

Again he smiled, and I wished he wouldn't. In another life, Rourke must have made a very successful cobra.

'Then maybe you wouldn't mind explaining,' he suggested, 'just why it was you marched into the library half an hour back and asked for books on this subject you don't know anything about?'

'Certainly,' I laughed. 'For the reason you gave. If I knew anything about it, I wouldn't have to ask for books, would I?'

'No.' He wagged his great head solemnly. 'No, that would sort of explain that, wouldn't it?'

'It would.'

But I knew he wasn't going to give up that easily.

'Just one little thing isn't quite clear yet,' he persisted. 'Why did you want the books in the first place?'

'Well, I'll tell you,' I said frankly. 'There's a whole lot of things in this world I know nothing about. In fact, the more I look at myself, the more subjects I find on which I'm about as knowledgeable as a cannibal.'

'That much I already know,' he said nastily.

But I was going well now, and I wouldn't let him ruffle me.

'So a few weeks back, I got to thinking. I pay all these taxes, and I don't seem to see much for it all. Here we have this fine library I'm paying for. Why don't I just get down there and spend an hour now and then improving, as they say, my mind.'

'The culture bit?' he guffawed. 'You? And how did you come to start with this nu — nu — with the coins?'

'Oh, but I didn't,' I contradicted swiftly. 'I've been down there, let's see, four times now. Last week I did ceramics, before that it was stamps — '

'Wait a minute,' he cut in. 'So you've been using the reference section for a few weeks, now?'

'Sure,' I said innocently.

'Preston, don't think I consider you very bright, because I don't. But even you can find your way round that section after three or four visits, no?'

This was what I'd been leading up to.

'Certainly.'

'Ah, hah,' he said triumphantly. 'So why was it necessary for you to ask the way today?'

'Is that what's been bothering you?' I asked innocently. 'There wasn't any necessity at all. It was just an excuse to talk to that little blonde librarian down there. That one has a figure — '

'I don't want to hear about it. I might have known it would be something like that,' he told me disgustedly.

And that answer satisfied him, as I was hoping it would. Where I'm concerned, Rourke will believe a lot of things if there's a dame somewhere in the background. With him, it would be consistent with his estimate of my character and habits.

He sighed heavily, and frowned. He wasn't happy about it. He would much have preferred to find some link between me and the McKern kill, but he was threshing in the dark now.

'Some day,' he promised, 'we are going to get some new legislation here in the state. Some new morality laws. And we are going to have our lovely new jails full of a whole lot of lovely people like you.'

'Are you through with me?'

'Yes, I'm through for now. But be warned, Preston. If I catch you holding out on me over this murder, I am going to put you away.'

'Thanks.'

I went back out into the street. The interview had served two purposes. First of all it worried me, because it meant Rourke would be keeping his eyes open where I was concerned. The second thing was that Rourke somehow knew there was a connection between the late McKern and old coins. It was obvious he had left word with the people at the library that if anybody started using that particular section he was to be informed. That was why Bubble-Cut had looked taken aback when I first spoke to her. Taken all around it was an encouragement. If Rourke knew something then there was something to be known. And if there was something to be known, then with reasonable luck, I might get to know it.

As I headed back to Parkside to clean up, I had plenty to think about.

4

Around eight-thirty that evening I left the heap a block away and walked a few hundred yards to the Piute Hotel. One reason I did that was because I didn't want to arrive outside the dump in a car. This would mark me as a man of wealth and position. At the Piute anybody with ten dollars is a man of wealth and position. I walked wide of the darkened doorways where only the occasional glow of a cigaret announced that there were others alive in town besides me.

I reached the dim-lit exterior of the faded rat-trap that called itself a hotel. A broken neon sign swung crazily over the door. It said P-U — H — EL and that seemed to restore a little of my faith in the workings of the world. I opened the door and went in.

There must have been a time when there was a reception desk and a small lobby, with maybe lounges leading off.

That time was gone. Where the reception desk would have been was now a long flat bar counter, and all the interior walls had been demolished. The whole place looked like a cow-town bar in a low-budget Western. Broken wooden tables scattered around, with aged chairs I wouldn't have trusted with my weight. If there had ever been any paint in the Piute, it had long since curled up and died, and once I caught my first whiff of the atmosphere I could understand its point of view. The place stank of cheap wine and tobacco, and sweat and dirt and hopelessness. There wasn't much action around the old town tonight. Two men in grimy under-shirts sat in a corner, chairs tilted back against the wall. They hardly spared me a glance, both staring into space engrossed in private dreams.

The other one noticed me, though, the one behind the bar. He noticed me come in and he kept on noticing all the way up to the counter. When I reached him, he picked up a stained glass and began rubbing at it in a desultory fashion with a rag he took from his hip pocket.

'I'll take whisky if there is any,' I told him.

There was no bottle on view, except a few selections of a special throat varnish which is the particular addiction of the local winos. The bar jockey hesitated, looked me over once again, then reached down under the counter and came up with a bottle. I looked at it and shuddered.

'Take it or leave it, Jack. This ain't the Ritz.'

I nodded and he poured a slug of the stuff. It was probably only my imagination that made me think I saw fumes rising from the amber liquid.

'Fif — ' he began, then hastily corrected himself. 'Twenty cents.'

I plunked down a quarter and waited for change. He didn't seem in any hurry to give it to me. I snapped my fingers impatiently and, after a long think, he came up with a nickel. In the cracked mirror behind him I watched the two dreamers. Neither one had moved.

'Nice place you got here,' I said chattily.

The bartender put his head on one side and inspected me carefully. Then he bent his head to continue fouling up the glass with the evil-looking rag. He was an ugly man, not made any more handsome by the jagged scar which ran around one cheek in a half-circle. At some time in his interesting life, this guy had made somebody mad enough to put a broken glass in his face. But ugly or not, I didn't want to look at the top of his greasy head, where gray scalp peeked out from the sparse hair.

I took up the drink and sniffed at it. A tear sprang from the eye that caught the worst of the fumes. The nickel still lay where the talkative barman had laid it. Carefully, I tipped some of the whisky onto the coin, and waited. Despite himself, the other man couldn't resist taking a look. Whatever it was I was supposed to be pouring down my inside began to attack the metal. Small bubbles frothed at the outer ring of the liquid.

'Nice place,' I repeated. 'Good whisky, too.'

The dreamers continued to stare into space.

'You got what you paid for,' intoned the other. 'You don't like it, there's other bars.'

'But I do like it,' I protested. 'I like it fine here.'

He grunted, still watching the five-cent piece.

'I'm looking for somebody,' I informed him.

'Zasso? I ain't seen him,' he replied.

I chuckled.

'How do you know, ugly man? I didn't tell you who it was I'm looking for.'

He scowled, and the scar stood out vividly.

'Don't call names, Jack. That ain't polite. And I don't care who you're looking for I ain't seen him. I ain't seen nobody in years. Ask anybody. I got the worst memory in town. And you watch your tongue.'

'Oh, I am, I am,' I assured him. 'I'm taking good care of it. See the way I don't get it fouled up with this muck?'

He didn't like me at all, but he was

puzzled. He didn't see why I should want to go in the place making a lot of noise. I was a stranger. I leaned forward confidentially.

'Listen, how'd you like to make ten for yourself?'

'I can't do nothing with a memory like this.'

I pulled out two fives, and snapped them with my fingers. He looked at the bills like a man hypnotised, then shook his head.

'Nothin',' he said.

'Tell you what I'll do. I'll double the ante,' I offered. 'I'll make it twenty. Look.'

I put two more fives with the others, all spread out like a pretty fan.

'This guy you want to find,' he muttered. 'Maybe I don't know him.'

'Maybe. Twenty bucks.'

'Does he have a name?'

'Sure. I don't know what he calls himself around this burg. But his real name is McKern, Toots McKern. Mean anything?'

He pulled his eyes away from the money, and looked at me solemnly.

'What's it, a rib?' he demanded.

I looked puzzled.

'A rib? What's funny about twenty dollars just to locate somebody?'

'H'm.'

He ran a thick tongue down over his unshaven mouth. He was ugly all right.

'From outa town, huh? Come far?'

'Far enough. What's it to you?'

'Nothin', nothin'. So you want to find this — er — McKern you say?'

'McKern, I say,' I confirmed.

'I tell you where to find him, and I get the twenty. Right?'

'Right.'

He began to chuckle. It was not a pleasant sound. Out loud, he said,

'I tell you where to find Toots McKern, and you give me twenty bucks. That's the deal, right? No matter where he is?'

'That's the deal,' I repeated.

There was a sudden slam from the corner as one of the dreamers let his chair down suddenly. The bartender looked quickly across, and the laughter died in his throat.

'You said that too loud, Leo.'

The dreamer didn't look so dreamy any more. He unwound himself and stood up, a thin gangling character with a thin reedy voice. He hooked his thumbs in the top of his stained pants and shuffled over. The bartender had gone very quiet. Skinny tut-tutted at him reprovingly.

'You don't never learn, Leo. That's why you're just a nothing guy in a nothing bar. You see mister,' he turned to me, 'the trouble with Leo, he's got to be flapping his gums all the time. Know what I mean.'

I looked into the hollow face with the wide glazed eyes. This one could be hard to get along with, I decided.

'He hasn't had a chance to flap them,' I said evenly. 'Every time old Leo here starts to say something, noisy people keep interrupting.'

Hollow-face stared at me quizzically.

'But that's just exactly what I mean about Leo, mister. He's gotta be sounding off all the time. Now if Leo had kept his mouth shut, he could most likely have found out what you want to know, and kept all that lovely money to hisself. Now

113

see what he went and did. He done went and told the whole town. Now, I'm putting it to you, mister, is that sensible?'

Leo stood behind the bar, gritting his teeth while his tormentor went on talking to me, not even glancing at him.

'Look, if you got something to say, get on with it,' I said.

'Sure, sure, I'm coming to it. Now, you wanta find this friend of yours, this McKern, O.K.?'

'Nobody said he was a friend of mine. I just want to find him.'

My tone left him in no doubt about what was going to happen when I located Toots.

'Oh, trouble, huh? Well, that ain't none of my business, I reckon. Anyway, you want the guy. Only natural you ask Leo, because he runs the place. But there ain't no special reason why Leo should lay into that gravy, now is there? All you want is the information. You'll pay whoever gets it for you.'

'Listen — ' exploded Leo.

'Shuddup, Leo, I'm talking to our visitor. Am I right?'

I shrugged.

'I want McKern, I don't care who tells me where he is. They get the money. Do you know?'

His eyes grew even wider.

'Me? No. Never heard of the man. But, I know where to go asking. I know where to start. You being a stranger and all, you wouldn't know that.'

'No. How long'll it take?'

He wriggled the skinny frame.

'Can't say. Maybe an hour. What kind of a looking guy is this unfriend of yours?'

I described Toots closely.

'M'm. That ought to do it. I'll get at it. How 'bout a buck for phone calls?'

I tossed a single on the counter, and bony fingers closed over it.

'Come back in an hour,' he invited. 'If such a guy is in town, I'll know it by then. And friend — '

He tapped a finger like a screwdriver at my chest.

'Don't forget to bring the money.'

I pushed his hand away.

'Fill your end,' I told him. 'I'll be here at ten o'clock.'

Turning, I picked up the rest of the whisky and poured it on the counter.

'Leave it there,' I told Leo. 'I want to see if it eats a hole.'

They watched me go out. Hollow-face laughed as the door closed. I walked quickly back to the car. I'd made some kind of a score, there was no doubt about that. Leo had been about to tell me McKern was in the morgue, and claim the twenty. Hollow-face would have known it too. If he was only doing what he seemed to be doing, which was muscling in on Leo, he too would have told me there and then. But Hollow-face knew more than the bartender. Or alternatively, he was quicker to see the advantage of something they both knew. Here was somebody looking for McKern, only McKern was already dead. It was worth a quick twenty to the somebody to be told that. But Hollow-face didn't take it. Because he thought he knew somebody else who would pay more for information about a stranger who was asking after McKern. So Hollow-face played it smart. He told the stranger to come back in an hour, which would give him plenty of time to tip off someone about me. If the someone wasn't interested, well there was always the twenty. He even borrowed money for the phone, a very nice touch. Hollow-face was a man to watch.

I headed south out of town on the beach highway for just over nine miles. Then a left fork sent me pointing inland again. There was nothing now but sand and rock and a few weary bushes wondering whether plain survival was worth it amid such desolation. Then a huge white sign announced that the lucky traveller would hit the Meadowlark in precisely one half-mile. The lucky traveller eased off the gas so as not to seem in too much of a hurry when arriving.

It was not much after nine o'clock on a fine warm evening. The car park was already two-thirds full and I parked the car neatly beside a brand new shiny Cadillac. People judge you by the company you keep, and the kind of company my car likes to keep is the Cadillac-Rolls Royce set. As I walked away I noted with disapproval one or two cheaper vehicles in the row. Some people are so pushy.

The Meadowlark was a far cry from the Piute. The guy who waited in the pine floor hallway with a welcoming smile was young and pleasant. He looked like an advertising exec. or the son of a company president. Nobody had pushed any jagged glass into his face.

'Good evening,' he greeted.

'Good evening,' I told him, just to show I know how to behave.

'Are you alone, sir?'

'Oh, yes, quite alone.'

He nodded. I was quite alone.

'We have two bars. One is secluded, and the other rather more social. What will be your pleasure?'

'I'm feeling social. I'll go listen to the chit-chat for a few minutes. Oh, don't bother, I know the way. I haven't been out here for a while, but I'm not a stranger.'

'Oh, fine, fine, I'm quite new myself, Mr. — ?'

'Preston.'

'Mr. Preston. I hope you have a pleasant evening.'

We smiled again and I moved into the big bar, the one that looks out over the desert. It's a nice place. Everything is smooth and relaxed. No waiters pushing you to keep on emptying and refilling all the while. At the Meadowlark, the management doesn't mind if you are one of those guys who just buys one drink and sits nursing it for hours. I went up to the bar and saw that all the stools were taken. I collected a large measure of Scotch over ice and found myself a small table by a window. In the far corner a small grand piano was being exercised by a slim negro with some of the most delicate fingers in the piano exercise business. He was engrossed in 'April in Paris', and I sat there listening with respect. As always, there were one or two people around who were talking too loudly, and I lost some of the quieter passages. It seems to me there ought to be talking bars and piano-listening bars. But I got most of it across the hubbub. After a few minutes a man got off his bar-stool, helping down the pretty dark-haired girl with him, and they went out. I slid across and plunked myself down.

The barman was somewhat different from his counterpart at the Piute. His jacket was snowy and the red bow tie was silk. He had an olive-skinned, almost fragile face, and thick black hair pushed into waves on the top. He showed me a lot of immaculate teeth, but I held up glass to show I already had a drink. He nodded appreciatively, as though he preferred people who brought their own drinks with them. Across from me a no-longer young blonde eyed me calculatingly. She looked as though she'd been at the bar too long already. In fact she looked as though she'd been too long at too many bars, too many places. I stared at the far wall over her shoulder and she turned her head away. I emptied the glass and looked thirstily at the greasehead. He glided down the bar.

'Your pleasure, sir?'

'Scotch over ice. Lots of ice.'

The fuss he made you'd have imagined he was preparing Pheasant a la King Henry VIII or something. When you bought a drink at the Meadowlark, you didn't just buy liquor. You got a corps de Ballet with it. Should that be barlet? It doesn't matter. I gave him five dollars and he made change. I peered at it as he laid it on the counter.

'What's that?'

'Your change, sir,' his tone did not alter. 'I believe it was a five-dollar bill?'

'I believe it was,' I agreed. 'But what kind of money is that?'

The steady smile slipped the thousandth part of an inch at one corner.

'I beg your pardon, sir?'

'That,' I pointed. 'That's American money.'

He chuckled politely.

'Oh, yes, indeed, sir, nothing but the best. We use no other kind here.'

I stared at him unsmiling.

'That's not what they tell me.'

'Sir?'

He contracted the slim eyebrows to make a query mark.

'I want good foreign money, like you gave my friend the other night.'

We keep the exchange low-pitched.

There wasn't anybody close enough to hear. The barman's eyes narrowed, but it could have been simply because he thought he was dealing with a nut.

'I'm very sorry, sir. I've no idea what you're referring to. That is the only kind of money I have ever seen here, sir. Perhaps you would wish to see the manager?'

'Better. I would wish to see the manager. Get him in here.'

'Certainly, sir.'

He reached into a niche in the wall, lifted out a purple telephone and spoke softly into it.

'The manager will join you at once, sir,' he told me.

He was as good as his word. Almost immediately a man appeared in the doorway. He looked quickly round the bar, saw me waiting and came across. A broad man, this one. Not so very tall, but broad. He was also getting a little tubby and I put him down as forty years old.

'Did you ask to see me, sir?'

He was affability itself. None of this, what's going on here routine. The guy was anxious to do me a favour. I looked at him sourly. Beside us, on the other side of the polished bar top, the greasehead lurked anxiously.

'No. I didn't ask for you,' I told the newcomer.

He looked enquiringly across the bar.

'Something about the money, Mr. Austin.'

Austin's eyes flicked down to the pile of change, still untouched.

'The money? Did you make a mistake with the change?'

'Certainly not, Mr. Austin. But this gentleman says it's American money. He says he wants it in foreign currency.'

The manager looked up at me with a question in his eyes.

'Is that correct, sir?'

'I don't want to talk to you. I thought he said the manager would come out.'

Patiently, he straightened up.

'I am the manager, sir.'

'Nah,' I scoffed. 'You can't fool me. Big Joe is the manager. He's the boss here, isn't he?'

Austin looked alarmed.

'Are you referring to Mr. Meadows, sir, the owner?'

'That would be the guy,' I confirmed. 'Fetch him out. He'll deal with this.'

'Oh, but I couldn't possibly — no, no, it's quite out of the question. Perhaps if we go into my office — '

'Whaffor? And why can't Joe see me? You mean he's not here?'

'Certainly he's here. But he doesn't expect me to go bothering him every few minutes. Are you a friend of his?'

I ignored that.

'Look, Austin, I'm keeping my voice down, because you don't want a disturbance in a nice place like this. You get your boss in here, or I'm liable to make a little disturbance. Quite a little. That'll get him out.'

He bit his lip.

'I'll take you to his office. I can't guarantee he'll see you.'

'That's better.'

I moved to follow him.

'Sir.'

The bartender called after me. I looked at him.

'You left your change, sir.'

'Not what I'm looking for,' I replied. 'You keep it.'

'Thank you. Thank you very much.'

Meadows' office was tucked into the rear of the place. We reached the door and Austin made one last appeal.

'You're sure you won't change your mind? I don't know what Mr. Meadows will say.'

'Don't worry,' I grinned. 'I'll put in a good word for you. I'll tell him you were rude to me.'

He paled.

'Oh, could I have your name?'

I told him. He tapped at the door, sighed softly and went in. There was an angry roar from inside, then silence. A few moments later, the door opened and an ashen Austin emerged.

'Mr. Meadows will see you now.'

'About time.'

I stepped inside and the door closed behind me. There were two people in the room and I didn't get to the man right off. First there was a girl. She lay on one of those low sofas with a back rest at the end. She had the blackest hair and the reddest lips I'd seen in quite a while. She had lots of everything else too, pushing its way out of a tight yellow silk dress with practically no front to it. The long gleaming legs were stretched out in front of her, and she didn't seem too particular about how much was on display at any one time. She ignored me, filing quietly at her nails while she did it.

'You want to see me?'

Now I got to the man. He was broad too. Not flabby broad like Austin, but thick with bunched muscle right across the wide shoulders. The face was heavy, but not stupid. Nobody ever thought this man was stupid. Now he paused in the act of cutting at a vast cigar with a silver gadget.

'Madowski,' I told him, 'you're employing a bunch of crooks out there.'

The girl went on filing her nails. He removed the cigar from between his teeth.

'Say that again,' he said softly.

'You're employing a bunch — '

'Not that part,' he snapped. 'The first part.'

I pretended to be trying to recall.

'Oh, you mean Madowski?' I asked.

'You have the wrong number,' he whispered. 'The name is Meadows.'

'Uh, uh,' I contradicted. 'That is a name, but not yours. You're Madowski. Madowski, Joseph, born Pittsburgh, 1915. Migrated California 1922. Reform school for larceny 1928, two years. Carrying concealed weapon 1931, six months. Attempted murder — '

'Shut up,' he shouted angrily.

The girl laughed quietly, but didn't look at me.

'And you shut up, too.'

She did. I didn't.

'What's up, Joe? Did I get something wrong?'

He breathed heavily, holding in his temper. Then he gave a forced laugh.

'What's it, some quiz programme?' he demanded. 'What do you want? And where'd you get all that stuff? You some kinda cop?'

'Some kinda,' I admitted. 'Didn't the

boy give you my name?'

'He did. It was — um — Preston. Preston.'

He closed the fleshy eyes in concentration.

'I got you. Preston. You're the eye. You're that Preston.'

'Same Preston.'

'The door is behind you. If you go now, you'll be able to walk through it.'

'Tut, tut,' I reproved. 'Harsh words. And here's me all set to do you a favor.'

'From you I don't need favors. I know about you. You're trouble. It follows you around. And if it don't, you make up some of your own. Trouble I don't need. Beat it.'

The girl looked now. It was just a sidelong glance from the corner of her eye, but she looked. Probably wanted one look at me before I left. She needn't have hurried. I had plenty of time.

'You're making a mistake, Madowski. Trouble, yes. But I didn't bring it. Trouble was already here. Bad trouble. That's what brought me.'

'H'm.'

He was in control of himself again now. To let me see that, he snapped a table lighter into life and held the flame rock steady until the end of the chunky cigar was a red glow.

'I don't like trouble,' he asserted. 'What kind do I have, the way you tell it?'

'The worst kind,' I said sadly. 'Murder.'

She took a good look now. Then she stuck out a little pointed tongue at me, and winked. He couldn't see her face, but he could see mine. I kept it poker style. He didn't move a muscle either. He'd heard the word before.

'Tell it,' he commanded.

'I don't know much,' I admitted. 'It seems there's a valuable collection of old coins. It's somewhere around, I don't know where. Somebody wanted to sell it to this friend of mine. This friend is well heeled, he can afford to pay. The contact man was using this place for meetings.'

He sniffed loudly.

'That ties nothing to me. Everybody comes here. I'll bet there's three or four deals cooking out in those bars right now.

I don't know whether legit or not. That's the customer's business, what he talks about while he's here. Just so he pays the tab, it's no skin off my nose.'

'Then you won't want to be bothered with the rest of it,' I told him. 'I'll just mosey off. When the cops come you'll remember I tried.'

'Hold on. You're not through yet. There was something about a murder.'

I hesitated, as though uncertain whether to tell him or not. I was going to tell him all right, but I didn't want to seem eager.

'I don't want to be a nuisance if you're busy.'

He ejected a cloud of smoke from between his teeth.

'Never too busy to gab it up with an old friend. Tell it.'

'The contact for this property was by the name of McKern. You may just recall they fished him out of the water the other day.'

'So? I still ain't heard nothin' that ties me in.'

'Try this. The bar jockey out there,

the greasehead. He was working with McKern.'

His face went grim.

'There's more.'

'Yes. This employee of yours, he gave one of these valuable coins to my friend.'

'Gave? Did you say gave?'

'Sure. It was a come-on, you know. My friend is a very honest character. The coin was kind of a sample. If he didn't want to buy, he would give it back.'

The man behind the desk frowned.

'Even suppose you're right, that's not my fault. I hire all kinds of people. They get in trouble, they do it on their own. It don't have to connect up with me.'

'Right,' I agreed. 'But this was in your own place. Fencing right in your own backyard. With your record, who's going to believe you-'

'Ah,' he waved a derogatory fist. 'You're bluffin'. The county boys know me. They know I don't pull that stuff. If you got nothin' else to say, the door's in the same place.'

'You may have the Monkton County

Sheriff in your pocket, but this isn't county business.'

'The Meadowlark is right square in the sheriff's territory,' he barked. 'Why do you think I put it here? Any fencing going on here, he'll investigate it, he'll catch the boys responsible. He won't drag me in.'

My turn to hold up a hand.

'Whoa. Too fast. We're not talking about the fencing. We're talking about murder. And that is city business. Rourke business.'

He thought for a moment. Then

'So what? He can't come outside the limits without the sheriff's say-so.'

'Correct,' I agreed. 'But the sheriff would have to have a hole in his head to try and stop him when it's a murder investigation. The voters might get curious.'

Grey ash fell from the end of the cigar on to his sleeve. He let it lay.

'So Rourke comes. All right, I know he's a tough one. A mean man. But he can't connect me up with some killing I know nothing about. Not even Rourke.'

'That he can't,' I conceded. 'And he

wouldn't try. But he's very thorough. He looks at everything, everybody. He'd find out things.'

'There's nothin' to find out,' said Meadows slowly.

'Oh, sure there is,' I replied. 'Sure there is. You know, you spend too much time in the office. You want to get out and around, see what's going on.'

'Such as like what?' he demanded.

'We won't mention the fencing. Let's say you really don't know about that. But upstairs there's a room. It has a wheel in it, among other things. This may be a big operation, but you should have noticed the room.'

'Don't know a thing about it.'

'Then there's the girls. Your captain out there, Salvatore, he sends your customers to some of the most expensive gals in town. And I do mean in Monkton City. The talk is he does it on your instructions.'

'Is that what they say?'

But he wasn't so sure any longer. Less aggressive.

'That's what they say,' I assured him.

'Try looking at it from a cop's point of view. An honest cop. Here he has a connection with a murder, a little stolen property, little gaming, more than a little prostitution. And all operating from a place run by a guy with a record as long as his arm. If you were that cop, don't you think you might get a little steamed up over an assortment like that?'

Clouds of smoke bloomed all around him. He swivelled his head towards the girl.

'You. Get out. Grab a smoke some place. And keep out of the bars, you hear?'

She unwound the long beautiful legs, and stood up. There was a little patting here, a smoothing there while she straightened her dress. I know places where the cover charge is twenty bucks for a worse show. She looked across to be sure I was catching the act. I wouldn't have missed it for worlds. She gave me a long and languorous look then made her exit. It was a genuine bump and grind performance. And she didn't look at him once.

'Nice,' I observed appreciatively.

'That's my wife,' he surprised me. 'So I don't need to say any more.'

'Correct. Why did you send her out?'

'Because up to now she hasn't heard anything. Now you and me are gonna do business. And I don't like a lot of people around. You stand people in a little wooden box in a court room and what've you got?'

'Witnesses?' I hazarded.

'Right. Those witnesses are a real pain. I like people, I'm very fond of people, just so they stay people. When they change into witnesses they give me the hives.'

I felt around for a cigarette and lit it.

'What kind of business do you have in mind? Will I need a friend?'

He laughed.

'Nah. That muscle routine, I don't use that. Years ago was different. I was a little guy them days. Little guys have to keep shoving all the time, so people don't forget they're around. Relax, sit down if you want.'

I wanted. I sat where his wife had been and drank in the perfume. Meadows went on with his philosophy of life.

'These days I got it big. I could bust you in the mouth a couple times, have you dumped out in the desert some place. What would it get me? You'd be sore, might try to do something about it. Then I'd have to do something else about you, like for instance something permanent. It's what people call a vicious circle, you know?'

I'd go along with the vicious.

'You were talking about some business?' I suggested.

'Sure, sure. Well, you come in here talking all this stuff. You're a guy who figures things out, you're smart. I don't know what that creep out there has been doing, I'm clean on that. But those other little things you mentioned, well now, I'd be lying if I told you they were nothing to do with me. So what have we got?'

'I'll buy.'

'We got this murder, we got this guy works for me, we got these other little details you dragged in.'

'And we got me,' I said ungrammatically.

'Right again. So what do we do? Here's what we do. I get rid of the creep. You can have him. You, the cops, anybody. But he don't work for me no more.'

'That's for openers.'

'Sure, sure, I ain't forgetting who tipped me off. With him out of the way, you got no need to bring no coppers climbing all over my joint. Except the guy used to work here, I'm out of it. O.K.?'

'I'm still in it,' I pointed out.

'Don't be in such a hurry. You done me a favor. I don't take favors. I don't even take 'em from people I like, and you I don't like at all. You do something for me, I do something for you. We're even. What do you say?'

I dragged on the cigarette and looked at him slowly.

'I say all I've heard is words this far.'

He chuckled.

'Good. Smart. A smart guy is a guy who knows when it's time to talk deal. Here.'

He pulled a fat billfold from an inside pocket, and spread out green paper on the table.

'Five hundred.'

I looked at it greedily. It looked good enough to spend.

'Well?' he demanded.

'It's money. I've seen it before. What is it supposed to buy? Does it buy me off?'

He looked pained.

'Aw, c'm on. Be your age. I know all about you. You don't make them kinda deals. And a smart fella like you, if you did wanta make a deal, I wouldn't offer you no lousy five hundred.'

'But it's on the table,' I reminded him.

'Sure it is. It's car fare. This thing you're messing with, that's none of my business. My business is right here, and my business is none of your business. All you want is the greasehead. You got him. You're doing me a favour. All right, you had to buy gasoline to get here. Five centuries ought to break you a little better than even. Am I getting through?'

'You are.'

I got up, went to the table and picked up the money. It felt as good as it looked.

'And this buys you nothing?'

'I told you.'

I wadded up the bills and shoved them in a pocket. He chuckled.

'It's a shame I don't like you, Preston. We could get along.'

'Sure. Now let's hear you tell the bartender.'

'Tell him what?'

'That he's through,' I explained patiently.

'Oh.'

He pushed a buzzer, and Austin appeared very quickly.

'Get that guy in here,' roared Meadows.

Austin disappeared like a rabbit. Meadows' face was beginning to work.

'How do you like that? A guy like that, right in my own joint. A cheap chiseller like that.'

He ranted on about the bartender, getting more and more steamed up. There was a tap at the door.

'Get in here,' he shouted.

The bartender came in, followed by Austin.

'Shut the damned door. I don't want the whole place to know the kinda people

I got working here.'

The manager hastily closed the door. The greasehead looked at me nervously, then back at his boss.

'What's your name?' demanded Meadows.

'Ruffino. Joe Ruffino, Mr. Meadows.'

'They tell me you swinging a little stolen property over my bar, Joe. Would that be right?' Meadows' tone was soft, almost conversational.

'Listen, I can explain — '

'Joe, you're interrupting me. That ain't polite. It also ain't polite to bring hot stuff into my place of business, is it, Joe?'

'Look, Mr. Meadows — '

'That's twice, Joe. That's twice you interrupted me when I'm talking. Come here a minute, I want to get a good look at your face.'

Haltingly, Joe Ruffino advanced to the desk. He wasn't in any hurry. In fact, twice he stopped altogether. Meadows stood looking at him. Then, quite suddenly, he swung a fist like a ham straight into the bartender's face. Blood spurted from his nose, and a cut cheek, as

140

Ruffino hit the floor. He lay there staring up at Meadows, fear written large on his face.

'Now come on, Joe. You don't have time to lie around on the floor.'

Meadows didn't vary his tone at all. He could have been discussing the weather. Ruffino scrambled slowly to his feet. His late employer smiled.

'You been lucky, Joe. You got off easy. I thought about having a couple of the guys give you a talking to, but you're lucky. How much did you use to make here, Joe?'

Ruffino was using a spotless handkerchief to mop at the blood. He made no reply.

'I'm talking to you, Joe. I asked a question. It ain't polite a guy don't answer when somebody asks him a question.'

'A hundred,' came the stammered reply. 'And — and tips.'

'That much?' tutted Meadows. 'I'll have to take it up with Mr. Austin. That seems an awful lot to pay a guy, just so he can peddle hot merchandise with the

141

booze. But I'm a fair man. Didn't you always hear everybody say I'm a fair man, Joe?'

'Yes. Yes, sir, Mr. Meadows.'

His tormentor beamed.

'That's better. Now you're acting polite. Yes, I'm a fair man, Joe.'

Meadows took out his billfold again and put a century note on the table.

'One week. Right?'

The bartender's eyes widened.

'Yessir, that's right.'

A second bill joined the first.

'And tips. Right?'

'I don't get that much in tips, Mr. Meadows.'

'You're getting it now. Now watch this.'

Meadows put down another bill. There were now three hundred dollars on the table.

'You know what that's for, Joe? It ain't because I like you, right?'

'Nossir.'

'That's ticket money. Use it to buy a ticket on a train. Use all of it, and one way. When you get off, stay right there. And don't ever come back anywhere around here. Because I won't be gentle with you twice, Joe. Kabish?'

'Yessir, Mr. Meadows.'

'All right. Pick it up and get out.'

Ruffino didn't know whether or not to believe him. It seemed too good to be true.

'I'll leave it there just two seconds longer.'

That brought results. Ruffino grabbed up the money. It brought him within Meadows' reach again. He snatched at the bartender's jacket front with one hand and lifted him clear of the ground.

'I'm giving you just thirty minutes, Joe. Then I'm gonna send a couple of people looking for you. Just to see how you're making out. If I was you I'd use them thirty minutes. I'd be on the fastest train that runs from Monkton Central.'

He banged the bartender back onto his feet. Ruffino didn't know what was supposed to happen next. He stood there miserably, holding the bills in one hand, and the blood-sodden handkerchief in the other. We all stood in silence, waiting for Meadows' next move. I took a peek at

Austin's face. It was blanched with terror. Evidently he was unaccustomed to this kind of activity, and horrified at his employer's winsome ways. Meadows spoke softly.

'Only twenty-nine minutes left, Joe. You're losing a lot of time.'

That galvanised the bar jockey. He turned and rushed out of the room. The manager made to follow.

'Just a minute, Austin.'

He froze in his tracks, and turned towards Meadows.

'Austin, I'm a little bit disappointed in you. How many other crooks you got working for me out there?'

'Mr. Meadows, I assure you — '

'Don't. All you have to do is listen. I'm telling you now, and it's a fair warning. Something else like this happens, you get the bounce as well as whoever it is. You might even get bounced around as well. You hear?'

Austin nodded unhappily, sweat gleaming palely on the frightened face.

'Now get out.'

He went out almost as fast as Ruffino.

Meadows breathed heavily and looked over at me.

'Satisfied?'

'Not quite. You said I could have Ruffino. Now you've told him to clear town. He's not stupid enough to stick around.'

Meadows snorted.

'I got steamed up,' he explained. 'A creep like that. Anyway you can grab him easy. Just get somebody down to the station. You know what really got to me?'

'Uh uh.'

'Him being Joe, like me. A guy like that, a nothing. Here, you can use my telephone.'

'I'll use the one in the lobby.'

'Suit yourself.'

I went to the door.

'Preston.'

'Um?'

'I kept my end.'

'Don't worry.'

In the doorway, a splash of Ruffino's blood had hit the sky-blue carpet.

5

The guy out front had been friendly enough when I first arrived. Now seeing me coming from the direction of the great man's office, he positively enthused.

'Where's the phone?' I asked him.

'Right over here.'

He took me to a small cubicle where a pink telephone rested on a white table.

'Who takes the money?'

He laughed as though I were the star of the Woody Allen show.

'There's no charge, sir, no charge at all. Just another of our little services for the Meadowlark clientele. Of course, you wouldn't be calling Bombay, I trust?'

I looked at him with a straight face.

'You shouldn't be so trusting. My whole family lives in Bombay.'

The grin wavered for a second, then widened.

'Whatever you say.'

I called Sam Thompson. He wasn't too

excited about hanging around the rail-road station. I gave him a close description of Ruffino, made easier by the fresh cut on his cheek. Then I told him to stay with the barman, take a ticket to the same town if necessary, and call me the next day. Thompson grumbled, but soon shut up when I mentioned money. Come to think of it, I've seen a lot of grumbling die under the same circumstances. I told him to call me as soon as he had something I should know.

After talking with Thompson I was going to leave the Meadowlark. Then a thought struck me, and instead I went back into the bar. It seemed from what Meadows had said that his wife had trouble staying out of bars. It also seemed he could be right. She was draped against the wall at a corner table with a large jigger of something pale in front of her. As I sat down she looked at me with a calculating smile.

'Either you have a lot of nerve, or you're touched in the head,' she greeted.

'Aren't we all? I didn't know Meadows was married.'

'You know it now. So blow.' But there wasn't much in the way she said the words to indicate she meant it.

'When did the happy event take place?' I pressed.

'Four months ago. It seems like four years,' she said matter-of-factly.

The way she told it, her marriage wasn't the romance of the century.

'Then why did you marry the guy?' I asked.

Her eyelids flickered as she looked at me. Again came the slow grin.

'You know, I like your style. I haven't heard anybody talk to Joe like you did in there just now. I thought the next thing you'd know, the highway patrol would be picking you up out there somewhere with a mouth full of sand. Now you come walking in here, trying to pick me up. What is it with you? Are you one of these guys with only six months to live?'

I picked up her drink and sniffed at it.

'Phew. Is there anything else in there but vodka?'

She shrugged.

'What's a girl supposed to do? I get

bored hanging around all the time. And that's all I do is hang around.'

'You could take a drive into town, see the sights?' I suggested.

'And you're all set to show me, right?'

'The thought did cross my mind.'

'Erase it. I don't want to be responsible for what would happen to you.'

'Pity. Still, if you ever change your mind I'm in the book. Under Preston. That's Mark Preston. Come to think of it, if you ever need me professionally, you'll know where to find me.'

The eyes narrowed.

'What kind of a crack is that? Why would I want a private eye?'

'Just making talk,' I replied. 'I guess it's a habit to do a little advertising whenever I can.'

I made to get up. She put a brown hand on my sleeve.

'Forget it, Preston. Thanks for the offer, though. Let me give you some advice. Stay away from Joe Meadows. That man is meaner than any snake you'll find out there. Keep out of his business.'

'Thank you, ma'am. It's been a

pleasure. By the way, I still don't know your name.'

She chuckled.

'You don't give up easy, do you? It's Norma.'

'Goodnight, Norma. Take that stuff in small measures.'

I left the Meadowlark and drove slowly down to the coast road. I must have been deep in thought, because I was only four miles from town when I realised the headlamps in my rear mirror had been hanging there quite a while. I reduced speed, they stayed where they were. I gave it some more gas and they scarcely faltered. So somebody was on my tail. It didn't worry me too much. If they were going to do something about me, they'd have done it back there on the country road, not waited till I was just a few miles from Monkton on a main highway. There's a bar and grill called the Sailor's Rest, don't ask me why, and I turned in there into the wide parking space out front. Then I got out, walked up the steps and went inside. Through a chink in the curtains I watched a dark green sedan swing in and stop. The lights went out, but nobody showed any inclination to enter the Sailor's Rest. I went through the bar to the kitchens out back.

'Hey, mister, you lost your way?'

A large man in a white apron accosted me. In his hand was a meat cleaver, and I never argue with people under those circumstances. I winked at him and held out five dollars.

'Somebody come in here I don't want to see. Friend of the wife's, you understand?'

He smiled broadly.

'Sure, sure I understand. And keep your money. I got troubles with my own wife.'

'Is there a rear entrance?'

'Sure, help yourself. Right through that door.'

'You're a pal.'

I went through and was soon flattened against the corner of the building, peering round at the sedan. It was parked so the driver could watch my own car, and that put it facing away from me. The moonlight was strong, and if the guy looked in his mirror, he couldn't fail to see me sneaking up. There was nothing to do but wait until some new customers arrived. I stayed where I was about ten minutes, staring up at the night. Somebody once told me there are so many planets up there, that the chances were very strong at least a couple of thousand of them supported life as we know it. People tell me all kinds of funny things. I grinned to myself. Maybe right now up there in the black velvet, two thousand private investigators were pressed against the rear walls of crummy bars, wondering the same things. It was just an idea, but I felt less lonely, and wished them all luck.

At that moment the diversion arrived. A big coupé suddenly swung into the forecourt, headlamps blazing. At once I left my shelter and ran the ten yards to the rear of the sedan, bent low. I was relying on the driver doing the natural thing and taking a look at the new arrivals. I was also hoping he'd be dazzled for a second or two by the glare of the headlamps.

I crouched behind the car, completely

cut off from his view now, and slipped the .38 into my hand. Then slowly, very slowly, I inched along the side. When I reached the door I came up fast sticking the gun at the driver's face. He was a stranger, a stranger whose face showed quick surprise but no real fear. A dark man with the kind of good looks that go big with the women. He even had a small black moustache.

'What's it all about, friend?' I asked nastily.

He looked at the gun, then at me.

'You have the advantage of me, Señor.' The accent was Spanish, the tone polite.

'You can whistle that in F, señor,' I told him. 'Now talk it up. Why are you tailing me?'

He looked as though he didn't understand.

'Following me,' I barked, in explanation. 'Why?'

He shrugged.

'To see where you go.'

He wasn't afraid of the gun. That's the trouble with guns. It isn't any use waving

153

them around unless you intend to shoot somebody. The reason I was holding the .38 on this character was only to prevent him shooting me. Once that little detail was taken care of, the weapon was as much use as an ice-cream in a turkish bath. I wasn't going to shoot him in cold blood, and he evidently knew it.

'All right, out of the car.'

He sat where he was, staring into the far distance. I grinned maliciously and leaned towards him.

'You think I'm not going to shoot this thing off. You're right. But if you're not out of there in three seconds I'm going to scrape it hard across your face. And if you think I won't, count three.'

He sighed and got out. I kept well clear. A car door slammed hard into your middle can be a discouraging experience.

'Take off the coat.'

When he had it half off I said,

'Hold it.'

Then I lifted out the small flat automatic that rested snugly under his left arm.

'Nice,' I said appreciatively. 'What is it?'

'It is Italian. They understand such things.'

Even without the gun he was completely cool. The Italians weren't the only ones who understood such things.

'Who are you?'

'My name would mean nothing — '

'Tell it anyway.'

'Ballenas. Juan Miguel Gilbert Ballenas.'

It sounded crazy enough to be real.

'Gilbert?' I said suspiciously. 'How'd that get in there?'

His teeth flashed in the moonlight.

'It appears my dear mother had much love for a movie star by that name. It was a long time ago. And she never met him. But I get his name.'

'What's the pitch, Ballenas? Who told you to follow me?'

'I am looking for something. I think maybe you know where it is. I am a thoughtful man, señor. If you know where it is, maybe you lead me to it, huh?'

'Who are you? Where do you figure, and what is it you're chasing?'

He shrugged.

'I am no one. A poor detective who looks for lost people, lost property.'

'I never heard of you. Where are you from?'

'Mexico City.'

I believed him.

'That's an awful long walk.'

'I do not walk, señor. We have a fine airline service. The car is only rented.'

'You came all the way from Mexico City to follow me?'

'Ah, no. Forgive me, I tell a very bad story. I come here to look for this thing. I never saw you before today.'

'What makes you think I know where it is?'

He gave me that infuriating shrug again.

'Let's see your papers. If you're a detective you must have identification.'

He pulled something from his pocket. Slowly, so I could be certain it wasn't a weapon. Ballenas had been around. I took it from him. The moonlight was just strong enough to show me a card not unlike one I hold myself.

'You didn't tell me you were private,' I

remonstrated gently.

'I didn't tell you I was not,' he countered.

'And you still didn't say what you're looking for.'

'Perhaps I may smoke?'

'Perhaps you may keep your restless little hands where I can see them. What is it you're looking for? I don't have a lot of time to waste, Ballenas. I'd just as soon bend this thing over your skull and leave you here to rest a while.'

'Very well. I will play this childish game. I am seeking a certain lost treasure which I believe to be lost no longer.'

'Treasure?' I scoffed. 'Even the word is a joke. We have all kinds of fast money around here, but the treasure bit is new.'

'I think not, señor. I think you know much that would interest me. I intend to find it out.'

His attitude was one of formality. We could have been a couple of politicians arguing in a crowded room. When two people are facing out in the night outside a bar and one guy has a gun, almost any combination of attitudes is likely. But formality is not one of them. This Ballenas was either a very cool cat indeed, or he was light in the head. There was nothing about him to make me suspect his sanity. I laughed.

'You're crazy, you know? Here.'

I tossed over the gun. He caught it deftly, looking surprised.

'There aren't any slugs in it,' I explained. 'They're in my pocket. Go on back to Mexico City, Ballenas. We're fresh out of treasure up here.'

I backed off towards my own car. He stood, calmly watching, as I gunned the motor and swung around in a wide arc heading for town.

The highway was doing steady business now as the evening traffic built up. Soon I was swallowed up in the concrete towers and canyons that symbolise a modern civilized concentration. Within another few minutes I was pulling into the kerb a block away from the Piute Hotel, in the same spot I'd left the car before. I got out and walked the dingy street. Opposite the joint was a two-year-old Cadillac, empty. That made me think a little. Not every customer in the Piute arrived in one of those, or any other way except on his two flat feet. Maybe the people who owned the car weren't in the Piute at all. Maybe.

I went around the back of the place, thankful for the brightness of the moon. The Piute Hotel could never be confused with the Brown Derby from out front. The rear was in a class of its own. My nostrils shrieked with agony at the unaccustomed barrage of assorted stenches. I told them to shut up while I located an entrance. There was a battered door secured by a piece of wire. I untwisted the wire and opened the door very carefully. Luckily it gave only the faintest protesting squeak. Then I was in the place. There was the murmur of voices up ahead, and with the faint light from a low-powered lamp high in the ceiling, I inched my way towards the noise. There were two men in the room, and I had to pull back sharply from the doorway at the sudden realisation there wasn't any door. At that precise moment neither of them had been looking my way, or I'd have been a gone goose. They were sharp dressers. Not loud, but just a little too sharp. And they certainly weren't the normal types who frequented the good old Piute.

'Listen, Rocky, we're wasting our time, I tell you — '

'Shuddup.'

'Rock, be reasonable. I told you this was a bum steer from the start. So some crazy man is looking for McKern. What's that to us? McKern ain't gonna do no squawking to nobody. This way, we just put ourselves in the thing. There ain't no need, Rocky. Nobody can put a line to us, the way things are. Now we go shouting all over the town. We might as well call in the Feds or something.'

There was silence.

'Smoke, I already told you twice to shut up. I don't want to make a habit of it. The guy's from outa town. We have to find out who he is, and what he's looking for. If we don't like the answers, maybe we gotta do something about him.'

'O.K., O.K. But don't say I didn't warn you. Anyway,' and Smoke sounded quite cheerful suddenly, 'the man said ten o'clock, and here it is nearly a quarter after. Maybe he won't show.'

'He'll show,' was the flat reply.

I was undecided whether to continue with the eavesdropping for a while, or let the two monkeys have a look at the .38 at once. Then my mind was made up for me by a third voice. It was about an inch from my ear, and accompanied by the sudden hard jab of metal against my ribs.

'Don't go standing out here in the cold, buddy boy. Step into the parlour.'

I said a bad word and moved into the room. Beside me was the skinny man who'd fixed the appointment earlier.

'Look who's here, gents. You got a visitor.'

The others turned quickly to inspect me.

'This the one?' demanded a coarse-faced man, whom I now knew to be Rocky.

'Same guy,' confirmed Skinny.

'O.K. Blow.'

Skinny looked hurt.

'You don't think I oughta stick around? You may need me.'

The other one, Smoke, laughed with scorn.

'Whaffor? The joint's already been swept up.'

Skinny didn't like it, but he wasn't looking for trouble with these two. 'O.K. I'll be out front when you want me.'

As he turned to go Smoke's hand moved very fast and a .44 appeared like magic.

'You got one of these?' he asked.

'No.'

'It ain't I don't believe you, guy, but I'll just take a little look,' he replied.

'No.'

This time it was Rocky's turn to apply the veto. Smoke looked at him in surprise.

'A room this size, you get too near a character like this, something could go wrong,' Rocky explained. 'He ain't gonna do any harm right where he is. Fold the arms, visitor. And if he moves let him have it in the knee.'

I folded my arms and tried to look harmless. I didn't want a ruined knee.

'That's good,' approved Rocky. 'I can't

stand hero characters. We'll make this quick and easy. Who are you and what do you want?'

'Name is Ballenas,' I replied evenly. 'And I want a man named McKern. Does either of you have that name?'

Smoke began to laugh.

'Shuddup,' snapped Rocky. He looked at me suspiciously. 'That's a funny name for a guy who looks like you.'

'My father's name,' I explained. 'My mother is a gringo. After my father died, we came — '

'Never mind the family album. This McKern, who do you want with him?'

'He owes a lot of money. Some people sent me to talk to him about it.'

They looked at each other quickly.

'What people?'

'People he owes money to.'

Rocky sighed and said coldly,

'We ain't making any progress, visitor. You talk nice to me and maybe you can walk outa here, free like a bird. Talk back, and you'll get a busted arm, just for openers.'

'Big money people,' I said tiredly. 'They

163

don't like interference from strangers.'

'Uh, huh.' Rocky sucked a thumb the size of a fat mouse. 'Where do these people come from?'

'Yuma,' I replied instantly.

'Uh, huh,' he nodded.

'He's lying, Rock,' exploded Smoke. 'I never seen this guy — '

'Just hold that thing steady and keep your yap shut. McKern is dead, Mr. Ballenas. How come you didn't know that?'

'Dead?' I echoed. 'How'd it happen?'

'He went swimming in the sea with a lot of lead in his back. Guess he drowned.'

'My people won't like that,' I warned. 'They like to collect.'

'But you ain't got any people, Mr. Ballenas. Not in Yuma, you ain't.'

'Did I say Yuma?' I asked carelessly. 'I meant Philadelphia. Or Vegas or somewhere.'

The fat thumb made an obscene plopping sound as it came out of his mouth.

'All right. I wanted to do this easy, but

I can see you're a guy has to be persuaded. Smoke.'

I tensed as he came towards me. There was an anticipatory grin on his face. At least I'd wipe that off.

'Turn around, guy.'

He was just out of grabbing distance. I stood my ground. The gun pointed downwards till it was in line with my navel.

'Around,' he said, very quietly.

I'd heard the tone before. It was that of a man getting ready to squeeze on a trigger. Reluctantly I began to turn. There was a swooshing sound and a scream from Smoke. Rocky and I dived together as the .44 clattered to the floor. I was nearer, and shoved the muzzle urgently against the thick man's throat. Then I backed off and stood up. Smoke was cursing and howling by turns, and plucking ineffectually at a slim black knife buried deep in his shoulder. In the doorway stood a smiling man I'd left in a car park thirty minutes earlier.

'Are these gentlemen going to help us, señor?' he enquired pleasantly.

'I doubt it, señor. We'll have to blow. Maybe we'll be seeing them again.'

He made a sound of disappointment, then went across to the yowling Smoke.

'I believe that is mine, sir,' he said politely. 'With your permission?'

He placed one hand against Smoke's chest and with the other plucked out the knife in a single movement. Smoke gave a sigh filled with agony and slid to the floor out cold. Rocky watched in silence.

'You take my advice, Mr. Ballenas, you'll watch your back. And your buddy there. Especially the buddy.'

'I'll remember. Let's go.'

We went out very quickly.

'There's a guy out here somewhere,' I said quickly.

'That is correct, señor. I have placed him in a garbage can. It seemed the appropriate spot.'

Even as I ran, I grinned. This guy was a useful character to have around.

'Where's your car?' I puffed.

'Behind yours, señor.'

'Follow me.'

There was nobody in view as we

reached the cars. We got in and started moving. I drove around for a while to be certain there was no one behind but the tenacious Ballenas. Then I headed for Parkside Towers.

6

Juan Miguel Gilbert Ballenas stretched luxuriously in one of my best chairs.

'Señor Preston, you have a lovely home,' he announced.

'Thanks. And by the way, I didn't get around to thanking you for what you did back there. Those guys won't forget you, you know.'

'*Puii*,' he scoffed. 'They are scum. In Mexico City we also have much trash of this kind. If I worry about their opinions, señor, I am already dead many times.'

'I can imagine.'

There was something about him that gave him an air of devilry. He was slim and conventionally handsome in his dark way. He had that knack of being graceful without seeming like a fairy. If I wanted to fault him at all I would go for the clothes. The lightweight brown suit was well tailored, but this man needed ruffs at his neck. He ought to have a rapier in his hand and a velvet cape. Then he would have been exactly right. Then I thought of something.

'Say, I didn't do a lot to help you before you turned up to help me. I told those monkeys my name was Ballenas. I'm sorry.'

'It is nothing,' he waved. 'When one play's a dangerous game, señor, one has to play it — er — '

'Off the cuff?' I suggested.

'Just so. In your position, I may have done the same thing. Only I would have included your address also.'

He smiled and I smiled right back. You could tell people would always smile back at this character, especially women people.

'And now, señor, much as I regret the need, we should perhaps talk business?'

'Perhaps,' I agreed. 'You go first.'

'Since I am your guest, I cannot refuse. First, tell me one thing. Do you know what it is you are looking for?'

'I know it's valuable,' I hedged.

'Ah, but do you know what it is? Have

you any idea how valuable?' I looked cagey.

'Valuable enough for somebody to bump off a man named McKern over it.'

He smiled again.

'With apologies, señor, I fear you are evading the issue. You must permit me to doubt whether you know much of this affair.'

I shook my head doggedly.

'This much I know. There's something very valuable involved. I've taken a couple of chances already getting into the act. Now I am in, and I am staying that way. Comprende?'

He looked slightly hurt.

'Please do not offend me with school Spanish, señor. I have some familiarity with your tongue. As to whether or not you are, as you say, in it, that remains to be seen.'

I got up and snorted.

'Forget it,' I told him. 'Just forget it. I am in, and I can be a very nasty guy to get rid of.'

'Pray do not excite yourself. It may well be that I shall need assistance. If so, I shall call on you.'

For sheer plain nerve, Juan, etc., etc., would take a little beating. But I didn't get mad. Instead I laughed.

'I have made a joke, señor?'

'You're a wow,' I assured him. 'There's two lots of people in this town looking for my blood, like maybe they want to spill some, and you tell me I might stand a chance as your assistant. Listen, Mr. Ballenas, you're a stranger here. Let me put you straight on something. This is my town. I know it the way you know your town. I can get anything done, any time. I know the places, I know the people. Cops come to me for advice. To me, you're the outside man. If you're half as smart as I think, you'll ask whether you can be my assistant.'

Taken all round, you were entitled to assume, I was a hell of a man around Monkton City. Ballenas listened very seriously.

'To be sure, some of those thoughts had occurred to me. But I am not a suitable person to be an assistant, señor. Anybody's assistant.'

'H'm.' I thought deeply. 'Well, here's what we do. We'll be partners. O.K.?'

It was his turn to think.

'I will think about it. To be frank, señor, I do not especially seek to make you my enemy. There is no need for this, and I have enemies enough. Will you tell me your part in this affair, while I consider?'

I made a face like a man who doesn't like parting with information, but finds it the only solution. Finally I made up my mind.

'O.K. I do a lot of insurance company work, you know the kind of thing?'

He inclined his head.

'A lot of people in town give me information. Most of it I can't use. Then a few days ago somebody tipped me off there was a big thing going on. They didn't have details, but they knew it was big. Then a hoodlum got fished out of the ocean. He came from another town, and his name was Toots McKern. It seemed a routine gang bump-off, and I didn't pay it too much attention. Then this contact of mine called up again. He told me McKern was mixed up in the big deal, and things must be hotting up. I got interested right away. Started prowling around, asking here and there. Somebody said McKern had been using the Meadowlark, and had some deal brewing with one of the bartenders. Guy named Ruffino. I went out there tonight, made a deal with Ruffino's boss, and Ruffino got fired. Hey — '

As though a thought had just struck me.

' — you must have been in the Meadowlark yourself.'

Again he bowed slightly.

'I watched your little argument with the bartender. I was interested in anything, everything. Then you went off with the manager. A few minutes later the manager came back for the bartender. I told myself this was not perhaps significant. Some trouble with a customer, the kind of thing that happens everywhere. Then the manager came back. I have seen many men afraid, and this man was afraid. I became more interested. The bartender did not come back. After a while I saw you in the hall, and I decided you might be worth a little more of my attention. That is all there is to it. No, not quite.'

'What else?'

'This other place where I followed you, and was able to be of some slight service. How did that come into the affair?'

I told him the story more or less as it happened. He smiled understandingly.

'Very good, señor. I used this trick once myself in another town. It was my misfortune that there was no one to arrive at the last moment. I had six stitches in my head on that occasion.'

A slender brown hand moved automatically to the back of his head, feeling an old souvenir.

'Well, that's it,' I said. 'That's my end. You never did finish telling me yours.'

'I do not think you will believe me, señor. My story is — strange.'

'I like stories. Try it out.'

'Very well. Have you ever heard of the Vicente Treasure?'

I thought about that and decided I hadn't.

'A pity. It is a most remarkable history.

However, it need not concern us now. The point is that a great treasure was lost hundreds of years ago. The place it was last known was approximately along the border between our two great countries.'

'How much is it worth?' I asked pointedly.

He shuddered at the commercial note.

'Who can say? Perhaps one half million, perhaps two million, three. No one knows.'

'Half a million is enough to keep me listening,' I assured him.

'The owner was a man named Vicente, a nobleman. Many have looked for it, but none has been successful. About five years ago, a man came to see me. He was from Spain this man, and his name was Vicente. He paid me money, he still pays, to be informed of any news concerning his ancestor's treasure. Oh, please understand, it is only a small — er — sum of money to show good faith?'

'A retainer.'

'That is the word. Each year he send this small sum, and each year I write a few letters to people I know in the north region to learn if there is any news. Always the answer is the same. No news. Until a few weeks ago. Then I receive a letter from one of my people. There are rumours. Believe me, señor, in these past centuries, there have been many rumours. But this one sounded promising. It spoke of Nordamericanos, hard men with guns. It spoke of a killing. I thought I should ask Señor Vicente if he wished to know more of the matter. He cabled five hundred dollars by return. I followed up the rumour, and much of it I was able to confirm. I was led to a man named McKern in Yuma. But I missed him. He had already left for Monkton City. I did not know this until I learned of his death. I came here and traced his movements. That's why I was at the Meadowlark tonight. I was almost at a loss, señor, and then Providence sent you.'

I looked sceptical.

'And that's all there is?'

'I do not understand.'

'I'll spell it out. These guys with guns, this killing. Is this a secret between you and me? I hear they have a police force down there, to say nothing of newspapers. How come all this stuff is kept so quiet?'

He smiled.

'Now I understand. But it is you who do not understand. You do not understand the people of the border villages. They love many things. Wine, music, beautiful women, the bullring, many things. But I regret to tell you, señor, the border people do not love the police. A poor man tries to increase his income by a little harmless smuggling, or perhaps he slips into the United States without papers to do a little honest work. And what happens to this poor man if they catch him, the police? Jail, señor. It is either jail or pay some huge sum of money which no poor man can ever raise. Always it is the jail. No, señor, they do not love the police.'

And I knew most of that was true.

'Maybe,' I grunted. 'But what about this treasure bit? There's nothing you've told me that says it's definitely been found.'

'Nothing I have told you,' he replied pointedly. 'But I have spoken personally with the boy who found the box. There can be little doubt.'

'Listen, for these risks, I can't afford any doubts at all.'

'Señor, for that kind of money, can you not afford a few little risks?'

It sounded like a fair trade.

'Suppose you find it,' I asked. 'What do you do?'

'I see that it is returned to its rightful owner.'

'Señor Vicente?'

'The same. And you? If you should find it, what would be your intention?'

I evaded that for the moment.

'This treasure,' I queried, 'it wouldn't take the form of unmarked used U.S. currency bills, I guess?'

Ballenas chuckled lightly.

'Hardly, señor. I do not know in detail what is in the box. However, there are certainly many gold coins all very rare and valuable. Some say there are diamonds and rubies also, perhaps pearls. I do not know the truth. Why?'

'It makes a difference,' I admitted. 'With half a million, a man could disappear and start a fine new life. I might be tempted to do that. But this other stuff, it would be traceable anywhere.'

'One could sell the stones,' he suggested.

'Sure, a few stones maybe. But when you try to peddle them in hatfuls, you are going to be picked up for sure. No, I guess a man wouldn't have much alternative but to give up the stuff.'

'And to whom?'

'Ordinarily I guess I'd give it to the government. But if you have this man who's the real owner, maybe he'd be the one. Did anybody mention money?'

For all his easy appearance, Ballenas had been quite tense the past few minutes. He wanted to know where I stood, and whether he might have to do something about me. Now he relaxed. I had reasoned the thing out in a way he understood. The profit motive predominated, and people being what they are, they always believe a man who is frank about his self-interest. I had passed the test.

'No one has mentioned money, señor. But let us correct that now. Work with me. When the box is returned to Señor Vicente, I will pay you five thousand dollars.'

Five thousand. Even at half a million, the lowest estimate, five grand was only one per cent of the total. As the value went up, the percentage went down.

'What's your end?' I demanded suspiciously.

He waved his hands.

'More,' he admitted. 'But since it is my investigation, and you do not have a customer, I think it is a magnificent offer.'

'I'll think about it,' I hedged. 'Tell you what I'll do. I'll work with you meantime, and I'll let you know in a couple of days whether I'm going to take you up. What do you say?'

The smooth face went very serious.

'And if we find the box in those two days? I am determined it shall go to Señor Vicente, as I promised. I would not wish to kill you, señor, but the box goes with me.'

'O.K. If we find it in the next two days,

I don't kill you, and you don't kill me. Is it a deal?'

He was still not happy.

'This is not a matter for the jokes, señor. Many men have died over this treasure. It is possible others will follow.'

'But not you and me. Not in the next forty-eight hours,' I insisted.

'Very well. I do not like it, but I agree.'

I held out my hand, and he shook it firmly. We had a deal. As I looked into the handsome face I was wondering for the thousandth time whatever got me into this line of work. What kind of an existence is it when a guy has to make a non-killing pact with another guy?

The door-bell shrilled. Ballenas looked alarmed.

'You are expecting someone?'

'No. And don't look at me like that. When I make a deal, it's good.'

'My apologies.'

I went to the door, slipping the .38 into my hand for company.

'Who is it?'

'It's me, Sam.'

Quickly I opened the door. Sam

Thompson was a mess. There was a blue and yellow lump on his left temple, and a jagged cut on his cheek. His clothes were torn and dirtied. He was leaning against the wall outside, breathing deeply like an old man who climbed too many stairs.

'I — I sort of fouled it up, Preston.'

'Get in here.'

I helped him inside to a chair. Ballenas watched while I poured out a large slug for my damaged visitor. Sam grabbed the glass and tipped the whole thing down at one swallow.

'Scotch whisky,' I complained. 'You're supposed to drink it. If you want to wallow, there's varnish in the next room.'

Thompson ignored me, letting the whisky spread its warmth inside his battered body.

'That's the best — the best drink I ever had in my whole life,' he announced solemnly.

'Your friend has perhaps had an accident?' queried Ballenas.

Sam turned blearily towards the voice, squinting as though he needed eyeglasses.

'Who's this?' he demanded.

'This is somebody on our side, Sam. Señor Ballenas, a treasure-hunter from Mexico City.'

'Oh.'

He winced and pressed tenderly at his swollen forehead.

'This is Sam Thompson,' I told Ballenas. 'He went to the railroad station to follow that bartender, Ruffino.'

'I see. I regret to see you so, Señor Thompson.'

Sam looked puzzled.

'Is he ribbing me?' he demanded.

'Take it easy, Sam. Very courteous people, the Spanish. I'd hate to hurry you, but when do we get to hear what happened?'

'In front of the señor, here?'

'It's all right,' I assured him.

He tried to sit more upright in the chair, groaned and felt at his ribs.

'I went down there like you said. Nothing happened for about half an hour. Then he turns up, the guy. That was a good description you gave me. I picked him out right off. Specially with the plaster on his cheek.'

'Say, plaster.' I remembered. 'I have some some place if you'd like to — '

'Nah. It's all right. Well, I spotted the guy and I figured it was easy. I wait for him to go buy a ticket. Instead he looks around, sees me, and comes right over. He says to me Mr. Preston sent him. He wants to see us both right away. Well, I wasn't born yesterday, you know. I told him I never heard of anybody named Preston, and he's got the wrong guy. So he apologises, picks on some other joe. I see the other guy shake his head. He tries one more time, then he looks very puzzled and takes off. I follow him, and he goes out the main entrance down towards that cab stand down on the left there, you know?'

I nodded.

'He sees me coming and ducks into an alley. I follow him, and there they are.'

'How many?'

'Two. I was half-finished before I knew it had started. One of 'em hit me over the head with a brick or something, the other one took care of my kidneys. After that I was just a punch bag.'

'Did you know them?'

'I don't think so. It was dark.'

'Did they speak?'

'One did, the short one, the kidney specialist. He talked all the time. Specially when I was down there on my face. He kept leathering into me and saying how sorry he was. He had this friend, he said, who wanted to catch a train. The friend was very shy, they wanted to be sure nobody bothered this friend. I got kind of bored with it all. I fell asleep for a while. When I woke up, there was just me and this drain cover I was lying on.'

'And no sign of Ruffino?'

'Sorry, Preston. I really fouled it up, huh?'

'It was bad luck, Sam. You weren't to know. Did they roll you?'

'No. Can I buy another drink?'

'Sure.'

'These men, Señor Thompson, you can perhaps describe them?' asked Ballenas.

Sam began to shake his head, decided it was a bad idea.

'Not worth a damn. It was dark.'

'But you must have obtained some

impressions of their size. Were they like this?'

Ballenas went on to describe with great accuracy the two we'd played our games with at the Piute Hotel. Sam listened carefully.

'I'll say this, señor,' he replied, 'when you describe a man he stays described. But that wasn't them.'

I handed him a fresh drink.

'You got a car, Sam?'

'Nope. I thought I was going for a ride on a train. I took a cab.'

'I'll get one to take you home. Drop around the office tomorrow.'

I telephoned down and asked the night man to get a cab out front. Thompson emptied his glass.

'Just one little favour,' he begged. 'When you come up against those two friends of mine, you'll write me a letter maybe?'

'I'll let you know. G'night, Sam.'

Sam waved to Ballenas. I saw him downstairs then went back to the apartment. The man from Mexico City was staring through the window.

'The man Thompson was unlucky, huh?'

'Not so unlucky as those guys'll be when he catches up with 'em,' I assured him. 'Still, we don't seem to be getting any place, do we?'

He flashed me those teeth again.

'You are an impatient man, Señor Preston. That is a good thing. It is good to want results quickly. But there are times when one must examine the progress made and consider the next move. I do not agree with you at all. I believe we are doing very well. Consider my position.'

I smiled as though I knew what he was talking about.

'All I had,' he continued, 'was the name of one man, and that man was dead. I also knew he was a visitor to this place, the Meadowlark. The past days, I have spent many hours in useless sitting at this place. Now suddenly, tonight, such a difference. First I find you. Then I have a bartender named Ruffino, two hombres from Yuma who will not be hard to find again. Then I have two further pistoleros, the ones who attack your friend Thompson. They may be connected with the men from Yuma, one does not know. Four hours ago, I have nobody. Now I have six people. It is what I call progress, señor, fast progress.'

'Six?' I frowned. 'Two at the Piute, two at the railroad station, Ruffino. I make it five.'

He bowed.

'You are too modest, señor. Also there is you. Six.'

'Me?'

'But of course. You have driven all these rats out of their holes in these few hours. You have a genius for making trouble. There was a story once, a story for children. It concerns a man who plays a pipe and all the rats follow him — '

'The Pied Piper of Hamlin,' I said automatically.

'That is the one. You are my Pied Piper, Señor Preston. You blow your pipe, the rats emerge from their hiding places and follow. If they will take the trouble to look over their shoulders they will observe someone following them. That someone will be — '

'Juan Miguel Gilbert Ballenas,' I finished.

'Just so.'

'Well, I don't care too much for your casting,' I admitted. 'But it seems to be working out that way at the moment.'

'It is working out beautifully,' he enthused. 'It has been my lucky night that I found you. And now I must go.'

'Go where?' I asked suspiciously.

'To bed,' he answered in surprise. 'It is very late. Today I have had much good fortune. You Americans have a saying, always cease to play while winning.'

'Quit while you're ahead,' I corrected.

'Just so. I will contact you tomorrow, señor.'

He went to the door.

'One thing, Señor Ballenas. You forgot to mention where you're staying,' I reminded gently.

'A place called the Portland. You know it?'

'I know it. Goodnight.'

I opened the door as the buzzer

sounded. I found myself staring at a beautiful silver blonde. She was as surprised as me. A light chuckle reminded me of my departing visitor.

'We have much in common my friend. Goodnight. Senorita.'

He half-bowed to the girl and swept out. Somehow in those two movements he managed to let everybody know he wasn't the kind to keep hanging around a couple of lovebirds.

She had recovered herself now, and watched him go.

'Mr. Preston?'

I tried a bow of my own, but it wasn't in the Ballenas class. Then I stood to one side. She hesitated, and came in slowly. As I shut the door I hoped my Spanish friend didn't have an option on all the luck in town.

7

She was tall, almost five eight, and everything else was generous too. The round face had gentleness as well as beauty. I figured a man could be a lot worse off than having this one call around midnight.

'C'm on in Miss — er? Don't take any notice of the place. I wasn't expecting anybody like you.'

She nodded seriously and permitted herself another couple of steps inside. Whatever else she might be, she certainly was not bursting with confidence at the moment. I put my wolf whistle away, but not where I couldn't reach it in a hurry if necessary.

'It's your call,' I reminded.

'Yes, I'm sorry. You must think me very rude. The fact is I don't usually — '

She waved a hand around at the place to indicate the kind of thing she didn't usually. I was glad the waving didn't include me.

'Forget it. I get lots of visitors.'

She looked at me gratefully.

'I'm Pauline Adler.'

The old man's daughter. Well, that put her in a special category.

'The unmarried one,' I remembered.

'That's right. There are five of us altogether. All the rest are married.'

'Sit down, Miss Adler. What is it I can do for you?'

I almost managed to keep my eyes off the long slim legs as she crossed them. Now that we'd broken the ice she was more relaxed. I hope she'd go on getting more and more relaxed. This was a girl to relax with. She wore a green tailored suit, rather severely cut, dark green moccasin slip heels with ditto handbag and gloves. Everything about her oozed money. I like to be around people with money, and the kind of people I like best to be around are women people. Especially women like Pauline Adler.

'You've undertaken some work for my father,' she stated.

'Have I?'

Her smile mocked me.

'You needn't be cagey with me, Mr. Preston. He told me all about it.'

'Really?' I didn't know whether to believe her or not. 'And just what did he tell you?'

'About this ridiculous treasure story. And the man McKern.'

'I see. It's true I did have a talk with your father, but as I understood it, he was going to keep the matter between the two of us.'

She nodded.

'Yes, I believe he meant to do that. But when I found out you'd been to see him, I faced him with it and he told me.'

'He seems to give in very easily,' I suggested.

'By no means. My father can be stubborn when he chooses. It's just his bad luck in this particular instance that he was up against me. You see, I have the same blood.'

'Even so — ' I objected.

'Very well,' she cut in, 'I made him tell me. I said I'd go to the police and ask for a reference as to your character. That soon changed his attitude.'

'I'll bet. What made you think of it? I'm assuming that you hadn't any idea before of what this was all about?'

'Not the slightest,' she assured me. 'But I know my father. For him to want somebody like you, the reason would have to be one that required no publicity. Bringing in the police, as I saw it, would greatly heighten the risk.'

I chuckled.

'That was a nice piece of reasoning. I believe I'm going to offer you a drink, Miss Adler.'

'Thank you, no. But don't let me stop you.'

I poured myself a middling ration and sat down again.

'Now that we both know what I'm doing for your father, can we get to the reason for your visit? Not that I'm objecting, believe me.'

'One thing my father promised was that you should know as soon as he heard from these people again. He has.'

'Good. That's great. Tell me every detail.'

'There isn't a great deal to tell. A man telephoned and asked if he was still interested in a certain proposition. He said he was, and the man said he'd call again tomorrow. The price would be one hundred and twenty-five thousand.'

'Ahah.'

I supped at the drink and pondered.

'What time was this?'

'A few minutes after eleven tonight.'

'This voice, did your father know it?'

'No. It was a stranger.'

'Was there any kind of accent, anything that may help in identification?'

'None that he told me of.'

I pointed to the telephone.

'Would you mind calling him and asking? He won't be in bed, will he?'

'Not yet. I'll do it right away.'

Her hips rolled smoothly as she went to the telephone. There was something here that didn't jell. If her father wanted me to know about the message, all he had to do was phone. There was absolutely no need to involve his daughter. I had a feeling there was more to come. She was talking now, asking him about the man. It was interesting to note the way she spoke to her father. There was a kind of formal intimacy about it, none of the little girl and daddy routine.

'Did you wish to speak to him,' she asked, holding out the receiver.

'Not unless he can help.'

'That's all then, father. Mr. Preston will call you when he has anything to report.'

She cradled the receiver and sat down again. I felt regret. It was even better when she moved around.

'I'm afraid he didn't notice anything unusual about the man's voice,' she told me. 'It was just ordinary.'

'That's the worst kind you can have with a deal like this,' I said sadly. 'And now, Miss Adler, there's something else, isn't there?'

She looked surprised.

'What makes you think so?'

'Because I'm a great detective,' I replied. 'Beautiful girl comes to strange man's apartment at midnight, with a message her father could have given over the phone. I may not be too bright, Miss Adler, but I can smell that one.'

She fiddled with the handbag, put it down.

'I guess it is pretty obvious,' she admitted. 'All right, I'll tell you exactly why I'm here. I want you to drop this investigation.'

'Ah.'

A look at the serious brown eyes told me she wasn't kidding.

'Could I ask why?'

The silver blonde head wagged sideways.

'I don't think that needs to concern you. I'm prepared to give you five thousand dollars, and that should be reason enough.'

'And what about the money I took from your father?' I queried.

'You may keep that as well. That's six thousand dollars for one day's work, Mr. Preston. Not every assignment is so well paid, I imagine.'

I finished the last of my drink and set the glass down with care.

'Is that what you imagine, Miss Adler?

Is that a fact? And what do you imagine about me?'

There was puzzlement on her face.

'You?'

'Yes, me,' I said acidly.

'I don't think I understand,' she returned frigidly.

'Aw, come on now, Miss Adler. It's plain enough. You're the one with all the imagination. What about me? Where do I figure in all this?'

'I should have thought that was obvious. You collect your money, and a very fair fee at that, then you quietly back down.'

Miss Adler, for all that million dollar appearance, was a little short on character analysis. Especially with that back down routine.

'And supposing I don't choose to — er — back down?'

'Mr. Preston, I'm not going to be involved in any auctions. Five thousand is my ultimate price. Don't waste your time trying to increase it.'

'Oh, I won't,' I assured her. 'Don't worry about it. And now if you're quite through, perhaps you'll leave. I have one or two things to do.'

She got the message finally.

'You refuse?'

'That would be what it comes to if you really boil it down,' I agreed.

'But why?'

'Oh, brother.'

I went and got a refill, conscious of her eyes weighing me up as I did so. When I turned round I said rudely,

'Oh, are you still here?'

She flushed slightly, but stayed where she was.

'Why?'

'Why what?' I countered.

'Why are you refusing my offer. I thought it was generous.'

'Well now, it depends on what you're buying. Take the case now before this court. Here we have one shifty, loose-living private investigator. You'd think a guy like that could be bought off for five hundred bucks, leave alone five thousand. That's what they do all the time, guys like that. Double-cross people, rat on their word, little things like that. They don't mean anything to those guys. It isn't as if they were decent people.'

She was interested but still aloof.

'Are you always so saturated in self-pity?' she queried. 'Or does that stuff make you maudlin?'

I chuckled in spite of myself.

'You have one hell of an ice-cold nerve, Miss Adler. Now, would you like me to tell you in clinical detail what to do with your money?'

'No, thank you,' she said calmly. 'But I'd like you to tell me why you won't take it.'

'I've been trying, in my curious way,' I assured her. 'Your father asked me to do something. He gave me money. I said I would do it. I will do it.'

'You could give him back his money,' she suggested.

'Damn it, woman, do I have to bang it into your head with a mallet?' I shouted, 'I promised the man, gave him my word. If he wants me off the deal, he only has to say so. But that doesn't include you. I'm working for your father.'

'I see. And you won't change your

mind? Even if I give you very good reasons?'

'Tell me the reasons,' I commanded.

She pulled the skirt further forward over her knees while I inspected the ceiling.

'I'm worried, Mr. Preston, if you must know. My father is normally a well-balanced man of fine judgment. But when there's any mention of coins, he seems to discard all his reason.'

'That's a failing normal to the collecting of almost anything.'

'Perhaps. All I know is, in his business life, my father would rather die than become involved in anything so underhanded as what is now going on.'

She waited for me to say something.

'Please go on. You have the floor.'

'All this nonsense about some treasure that may or may not have been missing for centuries. Why it's like something out of the Adventure Book for Boys.'

'Maybe,' I said thoughtfully. 'They pulled a guy out of the Pacific the other day. He had five bullets in his back. Does that sound like a boy's story?'

'That's another thing,' she ranted. 'The thought of my father, my own father, being involved with people like that. It's unthinkable. He must have taken leave of his senses. Can't you see what this can do to him?'

I lit an Old Favorite. I didn't offer the pack.

'He's a collector,' I reminded her. 'Once those guys get after something, they take a heap of shaking off. He's old enough to know what he's doing. And from what I know about him, plus what I've seen of him, your father is a man who knows how to take care of himself.'

'Against criminals, and murderers?' she spat scornfully.

'And private eyes,' I added. 'Or did you leave me out on purpose?'

'I've no doubt you have a very elevated view of your opinion, Mr. Preston,' she informed me. 'But what you think of me couldn't be more unimportant. Why else are you in this, except for what you can get out of it? Out of my father to be exact. Or possibly you're working for the other people as well. That way you could — '

She stopped talking very suddenly. The reason was because I slapped her fairly hard round the face with an open hand. Her eyes blazed with white fury, but the shock of it prevented her catching breath for a second or two. I went and sat down again.

'You mustn't come in here with that kind of talk, Miss Adler,' I said in an even conversational tone. 'A beautiful woman gets accustomed to saying just what she likes. A rich woman gets used to doing and saying what she likes. But when you get a woman who's both beautiful and rich, you have a king-sized problem. I didn't get too sore when you tried to buy me off like some third-rate ward heeler. I didn't even object to your snotty attitude, well, not too much. But that last part, about me playing both sides of the table, well, even I couldn't stomach that one. Now you just take your beautiful body, and your dirty little mind, and trot 'em both out of here, before I get real mad.'

She was completely dumbfounded. Rising to her feet, she cast her eyes around, unable to believe this was happening to her. Something, somebody would fly to her rescue. We both waited around for the somebody, but he didn't show.

'It's over there, Miss Adler.'

I pointed to the door. She gathered up the green moccasin handbag and gloves. Breathing hard with bewildered fury, she was very attractive. Even with the marks of my four fingers standing out on her left cheek.

'I'll kill you for this,' she promised.

I chuckled.

'Well now, that's the kind of talk I really understand. Lady, if you only knew how many people have told me that. And some of them were just a little bit more equipped for the job than you. Go home and get some sleep. Maybe you'll dream about me being strapped to a sawmill.'

She went then. If there was any lethal content in looks, I'd have been cold meat long before the door closed. When she'd gone I stared at the door for a while. The smell of her perfume was strong all around me. I reflected sadly that it wasn't the first time my temper had been responsible for breaking up a beautiful friendship. There you go again, Preston. Here we have this very edible person of the female persuasion, right here in the joint, and what do you do? Just what smooth seductive tricks do you get up to? The candlelight and soft music bit? Even the coffee and cigarettes routine? No. Not you. Oh sure, you can't wait to get your hands on the gal. Naturally. Only most guys in the same spot might have had some different movements in mind. Something slightly more romantic than trying to knock the girl's head off her shoulders.

I wasn't exactly cheerful when I hit the sack.

8

I peered blearily at the window. It was just dawn, faint red streaks of embryo daylight splitting the hazy east. My woolly head was getting around to puzzling out just what any of this had to do with me, when I got a noisy reminder. Somebody, some soulless somebody, was leaning on the buzzer. I said a word I learned from a marine one time and humped out of bed. After a good deal of semi-conscious groping, I found my way to the door. Gil Randall's huge frame nearly filled the available space.

'Tut, tut, Preston,' he chided. 'Not in bed yet?'

'Naturally not,' I snarled. 'It's an all-night drop, didn't you know? You better have some good reason for this.'

He looked as if he wanted to come in, and I looked as if I didn't want to let him.

'Draughty out here,' he grumbled.

'Good. Get back to your nice warm

office and let me get some sleep.'

He shook his head.

'I'm coming in,' he warned.

I set my bare feet more firmly against the carpet.

'Try it,' I suggested.

He chuckled and looked down at my feet.

'It wouldn't be any contest,' he told me. 'All I have to do is tread on your foot. Why don't you be nice?'

'Why don't you? Come back at ten and I'll make some coffee.'

'Uh, uh. Now. But I'll still take the coffee. And look what we have here.'

What we had here was a piece of yellow paper with a lot of official stamps on it. It worried me, but I hoped that wouldn't show.

'Search warrant?' I said guardedly. 'What would you be searching for?'

He eased his way in and I knew better than to try stopping him. Even if I took a chance on his great feet trampling on mine, I couldn't do combat with that yellow paper. I shut the door slowly, wishing my mind would turn over just a little faster, say about half speed. I was apprehensive too about what he might want.

'I'll just browse around,' he said chattily. 'You go right ahead with the coffee.'

Trouble was, I needed some of that black brew. After all, there was nothing for him to find, at least, I didn't think so. While the stuff was brewing I leaned in the doorway watching him. He stood in the centre of the room, rocking gently back and forth on his heels, a legacy from his pavement pounding days. At the same time his sleepy eyes roved around the place. Randall doesn't give the appearance of being too bright. In fact most of the time, you'd swear the guy was half asleep. That's the trouble with him. He has eyes like a hawk, and his brain moves at a tremendous pace. Even after all these years, he still fooled me sometimes. I would think he wasn't paying attention, or else he was relaxing, then suddenly he'd come out with something that showed just how wrong I was.

'Find anything?' I asked sarcastically.

'Just window-shopping,' he returned. 'Say, that begins to smell real good.'

It did too. I poured myself a cup, hesitated, then got another cup for my unwelcome visitor.

'That's mighty generous, Preston, in the circumstances,' he told me. 'Hot coffee for a tired old guardian of the law. Public spirited. Seems we got a lot of public-spirited citizens around these days.'

That was supposed to mean something, but I didn't know what. Randall gulped coffee and nodded with satisfaction.

'Good. You're kind of a handy guy. Some might think you're too handy.'

Again he lost me.

'What's it all about, Gil?'

For a moment I thought he'd fallen asleep on his feet. Then he said,

'I want you to cast your mind back. I know you have a terrible memory, but make a special effort just for me.'

'How far back?'

'Clear back to yesterday. The captain had a little chat with you, right?'

'It's coming back to me,' I stalled.

'Good, good, keep it coming. It seems we have this corpse down at the morgue. He used to answer to the name of Toots McKern?'

'Got him,' I confirmed.

'Ah.'

He turned the heavy face towards me and beamed with pleasure.

'Public spirited?' he murmured. 'So you admit it?'

'Huh?'

'You just said it was you got McKern. It's going to save a lot of trouble all around, and I want to thank you — '

'Whoa,' I held up a hand. 'Wrong, all wrong. I didn't say I got him in that sense. I meant I remember Rourke telling me about him.'

'Ah, pity. So we'll do it the hard way. They tell me somebody careless let you have a gun permit?'

'Right.'

'Let's see it.'

I dug it out and handed it over.

'Good, good. A gun too, so I hear.'

Without waiting to be asked I went to the drawer where the .38 lives.

210

'Take it out gently, Preston, so we don't have any misunderstandings.'

I stared with astonishment at the black Police Special in his hand. He looked apologetic.

'A careless copper is a dead copper,' he shrugged. 'I'm crazy for that pension.'

I handed him the weapon. He sniffed at the barrel and put his own away.

'I don't want to interfere with police business,' I said with heavy sarcasm, 'but what's with all the search warrants and gunplay? That thing of mine had nothing to do with McKern's death. I told Rourke to check with ballistics, they have the rifling identification. Have you guys in the department gone crazy?'

Instead of replying, he walked across to the drawer and put the .38 away. He stood there, a slow smile spreading across his face.

'I read a story once, about a man who had a licence for one of these. People kept getting bumped off, you know? And everybody knew it couldn't be this man, because they knew the rifling. But do you know what that bad man did? He kept another gun, one the police hadn't any record of. And that was the one did all the killing. Neat, huh?'

He was rummaging in the drawer while he spoke. Suddenly I had a nasty idea, but it was too late to do anything about it. Randall clucked with disapproval and the big hand came out. In it was the .44 I'd taken from Smoke the night before.

'Well, well, well. A .44 wouldn't you say?'

I stared at the floor cursing inwardly.

'Cat got your tongue? Funny thing, our customer downtown was wearing five slugs from a gun just like this when we got him. In the back.'

There was an edge above the banter now.

'Look, Randall, I can explain all this. Listen, you know me. I may do funny things, but I couldn't shoot a man five times in the back. You know I couldn't.'

'Is that what I know? I'll tell you what I know. I've been a police officer fifteen years. All that time I've been dealing with people. You know something, the more people I see, the more I don't know about people. And you're people, Preston. How do I know what you'll do?'

'But you *know* me,' I insisted.

He shook his head.

'Nobody knows anybody. Listen, I'd been a cop two years when I got sent to pick up a guy who was my own cousin. My own cousin. I'd known him since then, since we were four years old. All he did was steal a car. I figured I'd just talk to him like a dutch uncle. Know what happened? Know what he did, my own cousin that used to play baseball in my own yard? He put two bullets in me before I could get my own gun out. That's what he did. Take it from me, Preston, nobody knows anything about anybody. Get your coat.'

With Randall in this mood, there was no point in argument. I slipped on some clothes and had a quick freshen up. While I mopped at my face I said,

'Don't you want to hear where I got it?'

'Sure, naturally. But I can wait till you tell the captain. I don't have anything else to do.'

I knotted a tie and grabbed up my jacket.

'What made you come here today?'

'No harm in telling it, I guess. We were tipped off by a public — '

'Yeah, I know the rest.'

The ride downtown was gloomy. The sun hadn't a chance to warm things up yet, and it was cold in the car. Randall was a shapeless bundle in the seat beside me, overflowing all over the wheel. I was glad he didn't feel like talking. It gave me a chance to think about what tale might satisfy Rourke without giving away too much. I hadn't come up with much by the time we reached headquarters.

'Don't go running off now,' warned Randall. 'We'd miss you.'

'At this range?' I queried bitterly.

He laughed, and motioned me to lead the way upstairs. The night boys were coming to the end of their stint, and everywhere were weary yawning men in shirt sleeves, thankful the long night was behind them. They were lucky. I had nothing behind me but Randall, and a good helping of Rourke in front. When we reached the office the atmosphere was a haze of yellowy gray.

'You guys opening your own gas chamber?' I asked.

Rourke ignored me and looked at his sergeant.

'Well?' he barked.

'Right on the button, chief.'

Randall took the .44 from his pocket and laid it on the table in front of the Irishman. Rourke stared at it with grim satisfaction.

'Just like the man said,' he breathed. 'Maybe there is some justice in this old world after all. Why, Sergeant, you haven't offered Mr. Preston a chair. Please sit down, Mr. Preston. We want you to be very very comfortable here.'

Rourke polite is a side of his character he usually keeps well hidden. And it didn't bode too well. I sat down.

'If you're so worried about my comfort, how about sending out for some air,' I suggested. 'I'll pay.'

The blinds were jammed down as though to ensure none of the haze should escape. Rourke bared his teeth.

'There's plenty of air down in the detention block. As soon as we get through with our little chat, you'll be taken down there, I promise. Sergeant, would you get this little piece over to our friends, and see what they make of it?'

Randall picked up the gun and went out. I was still thinking about the cell-block crack.

'You don't look cheerful, Mr. Preston. Not cheerful at all.'

'It's all this politeness,' I explained. 'I'm not used to it, and I don't like it.'

'I always believe in being polite to the suspects,' he said smoothly. 'Let's talk about that artillery you had.'

'What about it?' I countered.

'Is it yours?'

'No.'

'Found in your apartment. Tucked away. I dare say it was planted there by someone who wanted to incriminate you. Would that be what happened?'

I yawned.

'If you say so.'

He tut-tutted.

'But it isn't what I say that matters. It's

what you say, Mr. Preston.'

I looked at him steadily.

'Here's what I say. That gun is my business, until it becomes your business.'

'All guns are my business,' he said edgily. 'Guns go off and kill people. That's why the good people of this city hire me, to stop that kind of thing. Be your age, Preston. Talk about the gun and I won't be too hard on you.'

I laughed.

'You're just bluffing. You don't have any cards, and I'm not about to hand any out. So long as the gun is clean, you don't have any reason to hold me. I think I'll kind of stick around for the ballistics report, then I'll get on back to bed.'

He wagged his head.

'No,' he announced decisively. 'It's a nice clean cell for you, whatever the lab boys tell us.'

'Really? What did I do, steal a hydrogen bomb?'

'Nothing on that so far, but we're checking. No, the boys on the next floor down have a warrant for you.'

The next floor down was the Robbery

Detail. I looked surprised.

'Robbery? Me? You have to be kidding.'

'Preston, it's not yet six in the morning. It's very unusual for me to make jokes at this hour. And it isn't robbery. Those boys cover one or two other little matters, you know. This is a common assault rap.'

'Common assault?'

There must have been uneasiness in my tone. Rourke smiled.

'Yes,' he confirmed happily. 'It seems you attacked a young woman. I know that's quite a normal daily activity of yours, but this one put in a squeal. And she can hire every lawyer in town to make it good. Do you want to know her name?'

Pauline Adler. She must have been madder than I thought last night. And the charge wasn't made out of spite, I was certain. She couldn't get me off the case any other way, so she thought a little time in the lockup was a good alternative. I thought quickly.

'But you can't shove me inside on a two-bit charge like that.'

'You're forgetting, Preston, forgetting what time it is. You ought to get around

218

more at this hour, keep in touch with things. Night court hasn't risen yet. It's Judge Richter this week. I can get him to make it thirty days at least. Specially as you're also a material witness in a murder case.'

He could do it too. My feet seemed to be resting on the stained and cracked floorboards, but they might just as well have been in a barrel of cement.

'I'm not a witness to anything,' I said doggedly.

'Come on, Preston, a little co-operation. I've always been very reasonable. Yes, very reasonable. You know something about McKern's death. You know it and I know it. The only difference is, you know what it is, and I don't. Why don't you make us even? Then maybe we can forget about the judge. You've no idea what his temper's like at this hour.'

If it was anything like mine, I pitied the accused.

'Are we making some kind of deal?' I queried.

Rourke looked pained.

'Deal?' he uttered. 'Deal? This is Rourke, remember. I'm the poorest captain of detectives the old Homicide Detail ever had. If I made deals, Preston, I could be living at some swell address. Like the Parkside Towers for instance. But I don't, so forget it. However, I like to bargain, like any other Irishman. I don't have any objection to a little trading, just so it's heavily loaded in my favour.'

The man had me, and he knew it. If I was going to get out of that building in a reasonable time I was going to have to give something. The only thing not settled was how little I could get away with.

'I'll be glad to help in any way I can,' I told him.

'Fine, fine,' he boomed. 'An appeal to a man's better instincts seldom fails. Talk about the gun for a start.'

'It isn't mine,' I replied.

'So it belongs to somebody else,' he snapped. 'Who?'

I hesitated. Not that I had any compunction about giving friend Smoke to the law. But it could hinder me. Smoke knew things I didn't, and I wasn't going to get them from him while he was locked up. If he got locked up that is.

'I'm waiting.'

'Well, there was this guy outside a bar last night. He was pretty drunk, I guess, waving this gun around, scaring everybody. I thought it would be a good idea to take it away from him before he hurt somebody. So I did.'

'You took it from him? And kept it?'

'Just till this morning,' I replied lamely. 'I was going to drop it around to the local station house later.'

The thick fingers drummed impatiently on the table top.

'All right, Preston, you had your chance. Let's go see Judge Richter.'

The door opened and Randall came back. He leaned across the table, put his mouth close to Rourke's ear, and whispered. Much as I strained, I couldn't pick up one word. The big sergeant straightened up, stared at me, then parked in a chair. Rourke chuckled, and began pulling a paper fastener around.

'We don't need his honour any more. I wouldn't insult a big-time killer like you with a two-bit charge like common assault. Let's talk some more. We now have lots of time.'

Randall beamed at me.

'That's right, Preston. Lots of lovely time to talk.'

I looked at each in turn, and didn't like what I saw.

'We do?'

'Preston, I don't like to leave a man not knowing where he stands,' Rourke informed me expansively. 'And where you're standing, all you can see is a big figure eight. That little toy you had, that's the same weapon that killed Toots McKern the other night. That puts you in kind of a jam. And that is not all.'

He paused for effect. He needn't have bothered. What he'd said already was having plenty of effect on me.

'There's more?' I asked.

'There's lots of more,' he assured me. 'You see, this McKern, he wasn't one of our boys. A stranger from Yuma. One of the first things we did was get in touch with the authorities over there. They knew all about our dear departed friend. In fact they'd been kind of wondering where he was. You know why?'

I shook my head. This was the time to be listening.

'It seems McKern had a difference of opinion with somebody out that way. The somebody got shot. In the back, naturally. Four times. You remember McKern collected five in the same place. Well, it seems those bullets in the other guy came from the same gun that finished McKern. So we have two lovely murders, one gun. And, we have you, don't we?'

It was time to think about preserving something worth while out of all this. The something I had in mind was one part worn private investigator.

'Hold on a minute,' I sounded worried. 'You're not seriously suggesting you think I killed McKern and this other character whose name I don't even know? A joke is a joke, Rourke, but let's keep 'em funny.'

He bristled at me.

'All right, you asked a question. Here's the answer. No, I don't think you killed either of those guys. For one thing it ain't your style to shoot somebody from behind, and for another you'd never have needed all those shots.'

As a two-edged compliment it would do for the moment.

'Then what's all this cell-block talk?' I demanded.

Rourke ignored the interruption.

'So I don't think it was you, but I'd never admit it in front of a witness. You have the gun and no story worth investigating. That makes you a prime suspect.'

I shot a finger at Randall.

'What about him? What about Sergeant Randall? He'd make a pretty good witness, or did you forget him?'

'I never forget, Sergeant Randall,' contradicted the lieutenant. 'Trouble is he's not the officer he was. He gets this trouble with his ears sometimes. Isn't that so, Sergeant?'

Randall cupped a hand like a catcher's mitt and placed it beside his ear.

'What say?' he grumbled.

Rourke beamed at me.

'There you are, Preston. What witness? I'm detaining you on suspicion of the

murder of Herbert McKern on the night
of — '

'All right. What do you want?' I gave
up.

It was Randall's turn to smile expansively.

'Do we have a co-operative witness
here?'

'We do, we do,' agreed his boss. 'Go on,
Preston, co-operate.'

I told them how I got the gun, and
described Smoke and Rocky.

'Professionals?' barked Rourke.

'If they weren't, they will do until
professionals are available,' I replied.

'Let me have that Yuma blotter, Gil.'

The big sergeant went to his own table
and poked around. Then he came up with
a slim blue folder which he handed
silently across. Rourke thumbed at it,
grunting to himself.

'Here. These sound like the guys. They
were buddies with McKern back in his
home-town. And very nice people, from
what it says here. Just the kind of visitors
this old city needs. Where do we find
these monkeys?'

He was talking to me.

'Search me. It shouldn't be hard for the department. Besides, one of them got a little cut in his shoulder. Could be bleeding up some hotel room.'

'Tut, tut,' Rourke grieved. 'Here's the city spending hundreds of thousands trying to pull in the tourists. Soon as we grab a couple, you set 'em bleeding. Want to tell me about that?'

'It was self-defense,' I said. 'The guy was holding that damned great gun on me. I only told you about it to make him easier to find.'

Rourke clasped his hands on the table and looked at me stonily.

'I hope for your sake this is true,' he warned.

'I hope for my sake you catch up with those guys,' I rejoined. 'Frankly, they're not the kind I like to have looking for me.'

'All right, we'll pick 'em up. Now, there's just one small detail. You may have omitted it by accident, but I doubt that. Exactly what has any of this to do with you?'

That was the sixty-four dollar one, and I'd been working up to it in my optimistic fashion.

'I'm looking for a guy named Ruffino.'

As an explanation, it was short. Too short.

'Well?' intoned Randall.

'Joseph Ruffino,' I amended.

'It isn't enough,' explained Rourke patiently. 'What is it with you and this Ruffino?'

I looked like a man reluctant to part with professional secrets.

'There's a guy in my trade down in Mexico City. He thinks this Ruffino may be able to help on some stolen property deal.'

'And can he?'

'I don't know. I haven't found him yet.'

'This man, in what you like to call your trade, does he have a name?'

'Sure. Ballenas. That's B-A-L — '

'Thank you. I majored in Spanish,' Randall cut in. 'What kind of property went missing?'

'I don't have exact details. They're being mailed to me. I gather it's to do with personal stuff, like antiques, maybe some jewellery.'

Rourke waved a dissatisfied hand.

'It's very vague, Preston. You always work in the half-dark?'

'Don't we all?' I countered.

Randall swallowed a chuckle as his chief glared at him.

'What makes Ballenas think Ruffino is around Monkton City?' he asked.

'Oh, he is. Or he was. Been working out at the Meadowlark as a bar jockey. By the time I traced him that far he'd skipped out.'

'So you went and looked at the Piute, why?'

'Not specially. That was just one of a dozen calls I made. Seems I got nearly lucky, because these two joes jumped me.'

Rourke stared at the ceiling, Randall settled for the floor. I looked anxiously at each in turn. If these two got nasty, it might take me days to get out of the building.

'What do you think, Sergeant?' queried Rourke.

Randall brought his eyes up from the floor.

'I don't know, Lieutenant. Seems to me this citizen knows more than he's telling.'

'Seems that way to me, Sergeant.'

'On the other hand, he did give us a good lead to a couple of people who could become a very nice pinch. We may get two killings cleared up at one hit. And it won't lose us any friends with the Yuma Department either.'

'Seems that way to me too.'

'So,' Randall concluded, 'taking one thing with another, I'd be inclined to turn this citizen loose. If we ever want him, we can pick him up in five minutes flat. And maybe he'll find this Ruffino too. Then we step in on that one, and make some more friends with the Police Department down in Mexico City.'

I looked at Rourke's reaction to what sounded like a very sensible summation by Randall. The grizzled Irishman was in no hurry to let me know his decision.

'How does that sound to you, Preston?'

I had to be careful not to sound too much out of character.

'I don't know,' I hedged. 'O.K. up to a point, I guess. But if I find Joe Ruffino, and he leads to a recovery of stolen property, I don't see why you guys should grab all the glory. There'll be a reward, I imagine, and that ought to be headed in my direction.'

Rourke shook his head sadly.

'Greed. Always the profit motive. If you want to get out of here, Preston, you better stack it up the way Randall says. And about that reward, just change direction, will you? Head it away from you, and towards the Police Benefit Fund. There's lots of good people who need that money.'

'This is blackmail,' I protested.

The Irishman turned to his subordinate.

'Did you hear any blackmail, Sergeant?'

Randall did the ear bit again.

'What say?'

'All right, all right,' I said angrily. 'I'll do it your way. But if this is what a guy gets for co-operating with the department — '

'Sh.'

Randall took me by the arm and led me out. Rourke pretended to be busy with some papers.

'You never learn, do you?' marvelled the big man when we were outside. 'He's doing you a big favor. He doesn't have to let you go with what he has. And you know it.'

'All I know is, you guys have all the cards, every hand,' I grouched.

'That's right. Only we're not playing cards, Preston. The name of the game is murder, and don't forget it. Something else you don't want to forget. Keep in touch on this Suffino squeal. If Rourke thinks you're holding out on that, he'll pull you back in on this one. Only fast.'

'And you'll help him,' I reminded.

He chuckled and gave my arm a friendly squeeze. It felt as though it had been hit by a freight train.

'Brother Preston, I won't only help him,' he promised. 'If I smell anything, it'll be me who suggests it.'

He stood at the top of the stairs watching me go down. I was glad to get out of the building and away.

9

Back at Parkside I put in a call to Reuben Adler. I told him what I wanted and said I'd be out to the house in an hour. Then I cleaned up, and went out for a large breakfast. A little after nine I was standing outside the big doors again. The formidable Emily admitted me, with no marked show of friendliness. Adler was waiting in the same room where he'd received me before. Although he appeared to be fully dressed underneath it, he was wearing a loose silk dressing-gown. It was a very odd garment, long and flowing, made of black silk and covered in gold coins and ancient pistols.

'You are very prompt, Mr. Preston,' he greeted.

'I don't think we have a lot of time to waste,' I replied. 'This thing is running out. Everybody is getting to be in too much of a hurry.'

He looked at me shrewdly.

'H'm.'

'Everybody?' he echoed. 'Do I gather you have been able to discover who these people are?'

He stared down his nose. I got the feeling he was embarrassed about something. Then he cleared his throat noisily.

'Not exactly, but I'm getting close.'

'Mr. Preston, what I am going to say may strike you as odd. I'm sure you have been to a great deal of trouble, and you may not take kindly to what I have to say.'

I'd heard it before. It was like a door closing, a steel shutter coming down. A pay off.

'I'd have to hear it before I could judge.'

'Quite.'

He let me hear him clear his throat, to show the first time was no freak performance.

'My daughter told you of the telephone call I received. Since then, I have been thinking a great deal. Believe me, I am aware of the moral issues involved. Nevertheless, I do not wish you to proceed in the matter. If you will let me know whether there is any further money due to you, I will see it is paid immediately. I have not arrived at this decision lightly, Mr. Preston. Indeed I slept very little last night.'

I laughed quickly. The whole thing was too ridiculous to do anything else. Then I helped myself to a chair. Adler looked at me in irritation.

'This is hardly a humorous matter,' he informed me stiffly.

'Oh, we agree on that,' I assured him. 'Mr. Adler, I know this kind of thing is not your usual territory, so that helps to explain your attitude. But you've stirred things up. Or more accurately, I've been doing that on your account. You can't just switch people on and off like lamps.'

'I do not follow your reasoning, sir. Surely, as your temporary employer, I have the right to terminate the arrangement?'

'Oh, sure, you have that right. I'm not trying to deny you your democratic right to fire me. What I'm telling you is, it won't make a bit of difference.'

He shook his head wearily.

'I did not have much sleep last night. I must trouble you to explain that a little further.'

'Certainly. You see, when you start an investigation of this kind, you get people moving. It's like turning a kid loose in a switchhouse. Once some of those switches are down, they stay down. You go ahead and fire me if you want. It won't change the course of events. Let me tell you what's been happening. You're entitled to a report in any case.'

He went and sat down close by the window.

'Very well.'

I told him what had happened since I last saw him. He listened with deep attention, tut-tutting at some of the nastier parts. When I finished I let him have a couple of minutes for it all to sink in. Finally he said,

'H'm. I must say, I seem to have picked the right man. You have certainly made a great deal of progress.'

'Too much to suit some people,' I asserted. 'It was their idea you should call me off, wasn't it?'

He stroked the arm of his chair thoughtfully.

'It was mentioned, certainly. Indeed, I was told that if you persisted your life might be in danger. And so would the — um — transaction.'

What I would have liked to ask him then was whether it was my life or the risk of losing the coins that decided him. But I didn't.

'Just bluff,' I said. 'Nobody is going to stop trying to kill me, just because you're not paying me any more. I know too much, and on top of that, these people have no idea just how much. They can't take any chances. There are already two murders involved. More for all I know. When you play for keeps, Mr. Adler, you play till the game is finished. Whether I get killed on your time or my own is academic, wouldn't you say?'

He shuddered.

'If I had had the slightest idea events would take such a turn, I would never have allowed myself to become involved.'

At that moment he meant it. He was thinking about people, and the things money does to them. But I knew his regret didn't go all that deep down. It was the collecting bug that had put him in this spot. A little more think about the people and the circumstances at the outset might have avoided the situation we now had.

'What's it going to be, Mr. Adler?'

He sighed.

'What you have told me is a complication I had not foreseen. I must think.'

'All right. While you're thinking, could I have a look at whatever information you've got for me?'

'Information?' he queried absently.

'We talked on the telephone this morning,' I reminded. 'That's the reason I came.'

Adler snapped his fingers.

'Of course. As a matter of fact, there was nothing for me to do. You asked me for some kind of reference book which would contain names of people interested in numismatics. Well, I thought about it, but I couldn't think of some easy way to help you. Then I remembered this.'

He held up what looked like a slim magazine. I tried to look intelligent.

'Convention program,' he explained. 'We had a convention just last year in San Francisco. Not a big affair, not coast to coast. Mostly West Coast people, but we had quite a few in from further afield. Could I ask what you hope to find?'

I took it from him, and restrained my impatience to open it.

'Certainly. I'm only ashamed I didn't think of it yesterday. I've been going on the assumption we are dealing with ordinary thieves. They may be high-class thieves, but thieves for all that. But I missed something I oughtn't. And it was you pointed it out to me, right in this room.'

It was his turn to try looking intelligent. I hoped my effort had been more convincing.

'I thought,' I went on, 'some guys had been put in touch with this missing treasure. They got the stuff, picked on you for a buyer, then started the auction.'

'You think differently now?'

'Yes. Think back to that story you told me. About how those three coins, the doubloon, the noble and the — the — '

' — bezant,' he supplied.

'Thank you. You told me it was the fact these three coins were together was the most significant fact about this whole thing. Separately they would all be fine pieces, but together they pointed very strongly towards the Vicente hoard.'

He wrinkled his lips disapprovingly.

'I am not one of those who subscribes to the Vicente family claims in this business, Mr. Preston. The correct name for this prize is Seldon's Gold.'

I wasn't going to spend the rest of the day arguing description with a man of such determined views as Reuben Adler.

'All right, Seldon's Gold,' I conceded. 'So here we have a boxful of old gold pieces, and in the possession of a bunch of hoodlums. They pick out one noble, one bezant, one doubloon. They've already picked out their customer. That's you, Mr. Adler. The next thing is to get the samples to you. Right?'

'Right,' he agreed. 'But I don't see what you're coming to.'

'Just this. Nobody knows what proportions there are in the box of each of these pieces we're talking about. But think of any assortment in a box. Dip into it casually. What do you suppose are the odds against coming out with three different coins? And those the very three which will convince somebody like yourself of the authenticity of the find? What do you imagine those odds would be, Mr. Adler?'

He nodded with enthusiasm.

'Of course, of course, millions to one, probably. I see why you want the program. The people who have the box are getting expert advice. They must be.'

'That's it. Either they're getting it now, or they had it in the first instance. I'm hoping one of us might see a familiar face in here, or pick a name.'

Adler chuckled.

'I'm afraid you'll have to see what you can do alone. I would only confuse the issue. I know two-thirds of the people at that convention either by sight or by name.'

I flicked the pages carefully, peering intently at the faces of the convention chairman, committee men and so forth.

There were pictures of the speakers too, at the many formal dinners on the list of attractions. Stare as I might, I couldn't find a face or a name that tied in with the information I had so far. Reluctantly I turned to the last two pages. These were a close-typed alphabetical index of all the people expected to attend. I ran my finger slowly down the page. And at once I made a noise.

'Have you found something?' asked Adler excitedly.

'I don't know,' I admitted. 'There's a guy here named Austin. Emmet W. Austin. He hails from Yuma Arizona.'

'Well, what about it?'

I looked at Adler almost dreamily.

'That place you went the other night, the Meadowlark. The manager's name is Austin.'

'Oh, come, it's hardly an unusual name.'

'No. But it isn't Smith either. Do you know this Austin?'

He thought about it.

'Not right away. Of course I might know the face.'

'No time. Could I use the telephone?'

He motioned me to go ahead. I put in a call to Yuma. There was some traffic and I had to wait a few minutes. Adler picked up the program, studied the name as though it might come back to his mind if he looked hard enough. The phone jangled. I told the Yuma operator the name of the man I wanted. There was only one Emmet W. in the book it seemed. I asked her to call the number. After a few burrs the receiver was lifted.

'Yes?' A woman's voice.

'I'd like to speak to Mr. Austin, please. Mr. Emmet W. Austin?

'Oh, I'm sorry but he's not here. Who is this?'

'I'm calling from Monkton City in California,' I told her. 'I have a most important message for Mr. Austin. Do you have any idea where he can be reached?'

There was a pause at the other end, and I distinctly heard a sniff.

'Is this some kind of a joke, young man?'

'No, ma'am. Why do you say that?'

She didn't really believe me, but she kept her patience.

'Because, as you perfectly well know, Mr. Austin is over there right this moment.'

I tried to keep the triumph out of my voice.

'What a lucky coincidence,' I assured her. 'Do you happen to know where I can get in touch with him?'

'No, I do not. And if I did, I wouldn't tell it to some perfect stranger on the telephone. What is this all about? First she goes gallivanting off without so much as a good-bye, then he goes. Next thing I know there are lunatics on the telephone.'

'Did you say Mrs. Austin is here too?' I asked.

'Did not. There isn't any Mrs. Austin. I'm talking about his sister. And I simply will not tell you anything at all. Goodbye.'

I looked at the dead phone in my hand and chuckled. Lady, you couldn't have told me more if you'd been trying.

'Well?' demanded my host.

'It's him,' I confirmed. 'It has to be. All right, maybe there's more than one

243

Emmet W. Austin. But nobody's going to tell me there are two men by that name, both from Yuma, and both just chancing to visit this fair city at the same time. It has to be our man.'

'But this is a great step forward. What are you going to do?'

He was all eager inquisitiveness. He was on my team again, playing detectives. But I couldn't trust him. At bottom, I was convinced he'd be unreliable if there was any threat to his ultimate possession of that certain box.

'I don't know,' I lied. 'First of all, I'm going to get some breakfast and think this all through. It pays to go slower towards the end, Mr. Adler. You go too fast, people think they're being pushed. And when these people get pushed somebody gets dead. I don't want that to be me.'

He was all concern.

'Why, certainly not. You must take every possible precaution, Mr. Preston. If anything should happen to you on account of what I always thought to be a harmless hobby — why, I don't know what I would do.'

That would depend on whether or not you got your hooks on those coins. I reflected. I wrote down Sam Thompson's telephone number.

'That's the number of a friend of mine, Mr. Adler. He'll be able to contact me, most of the time. As soon as these people make their call, let him know.'

'Of course. Is there anything else I can do?'

I thought I'd give it one last try.

'There is. Don't play ball with these characters. You can only come out on the losing side. Try to remember it, Mr. Adler.'

I left him then. There was a lot to do and time was running out.

10

For once I knew where Sam Thompson was holed up. Somebody once described Sam as an itinerant bottle with a work allergy and the description was too accurate for him to sue. Luckily he'd been doing a little work lately, and that gave him a semi-permanent address. It was just one room, and not a stone's throw from River Street, but it was better than nothing. I leaned on the bell for what seemed like half an hour before there were noises of protest inside. Finally, he slipped the catch and peered out.

'Oh, brother,' he groaned. 'My lucky charm.'

'Nice to see you, too,' I returned. 'Do I come in?'

He rolled away from view leaving the door open. I stepped in. He sat on the bed inspecting his aches and pains. Since he was only wearing shorts it was easy to see where he ached and pained.

'Good work over, wasn't it?' I asked sympathetically.

'You think so?' he snapped. 'Amateur night, Preston, that's all. Wait till I catch up with those babies, then ask to see their bruises. That will be something to see.'

'My pleasure,' I assured him. 'Matter of fact that's why I'm here. I hope to be having a little talk with those guys before the day is out. You feeling like conversation?'

He scratched at his head and frowned.

'I feel it, but am I fit for it?' he asked himself.

'That's up to you. I just make the bids.'

'H'm. You wouldn't have any idea what time this little talk will be, I guess?'

'Quien sabe?' ' I shrugged. 'Does it matter?'

'Oh, it matters,' he said decisively. 'If I can catch about two hours more sleep, I guess I'm in.'

Two hours. That would make it almost noon. I couldn't afford the time.

'Sorry, Sam. I couldn't hold up this entire deal for two whole hours. But

247

there's something else you can do. Something very important.'

Thompson sighed.

'Nothing is so important it could get me through that door under two hours.'

'No doors. You just stay in. Asleep if you want.'

He smiled now, the lazy grin that made him look almost homely.

'That kind of work is my specialty. What do I do?'

'You listen.'

I sat down and started to talk. I told Sam the whole trick, kept nothing back. Well, not quite nothing. I didn't tell him how much Adler had paid me. As I got on with the story, I found myself rationalising, putting untidy facts into apple pie order. My audience seemed to plunge deeper and deeper into gloom as I went on.

'Well, thanks,' he said, when I finished. 'Before you came all I had was a few bruises. Now you come busting in here telling me things I shouldn't ought to know. Trouble things. What did you want to go and do that for?'

'Because somebody has to know what I know, Sam. I'm just groping around. I have a few ideas, but they may go sour. If they do, I want you to go and give all that stuff to Rourke.'

He looked at me dourly.

'That bad, huh? Well, I didn't really want any more sleep anyway. Think I'll kind of tag along, protect my investment.'

'Investment?'

'Sure. You owe me one day's work plus a little extra something for plaster.'

I grinned.

'You'll get your money. And I appreciate the offer, but you're not up to it. Not right this minute.'

By way of an answer he stood up and began pulling on his shirt. That was all he did, was begin. After a couple of minutes struggling and wincing he dropped the shirt to the floor and kicked at it. Ashamed, he said,

'I can't even lick a shirt.'

'Here.'

I passed him an Old Favorite and lit one myself. He dragged at it and coughed.

'What're you gonna do, Preston? From the size of this outfit you better call out the National Guard. You must have mentioned about ten people already.'

I made a first-class smoke ring inside my mouth and blew out a thick fuzzy cloud. That's always happening to me.

'I think we have two organisations here. If I can get them fighting each other, maybe I can just stand around picking up the pieces.'

His face brightened.

'Sure. The pieces of eight.'

I looked at him in disgust and he subsided.

'I think Toots McKern belonged with Outfit A. I think he took off with the box and came here to Monkton. Then he either joined up with Outfit B, or they muscled into the act somehow. Outfit A came looking for their missing member — '

'And knocked him off,' supplied Sam. 'Say, that has possibilities.'

'Perhaps. There's another possibility. If Outfit A didn't know anything about B, then B could have eliminated Toots to make sure they didn't get spotted.'

'H'm,' he said doubtfully. 'After McKern brought the stuff here in the first place?'

'It's a hard world, Sam. And never harder than when somebody tries to take away something from somebody else.'

'Sad, but true,' he agreed. 'So let's imagine there are two different outfits. How do all these people divide out?'

'Ah, yes, a lovely question. I wish I knew the answer. Still, you remember what I told you. All of it. And by the way. Adler has your number here. I told him you know where I'll be. If he calls, tell him I said he was to do nothing until he hears from me.'

'And if he won't listen?'

'He'll be a walking target. A guy like him isn't equipped to meet characters like this with a grip full of money. Do what you can.'

I left Sam and headed for the Piute Hotel. On the way I stopped off to make a telephone call to a lawyer friend of mine. I had something private to take care of. When that was done I went to the broken-down bar and hammered on the door. It took more than ten minutes to get some action. Then there was a long interval while the guy on the other side of the door slipped endless bolts, catches and chains. While this was going on I was trying to puzzle out who'd want to break into such a dump, and what would they hope to find. When all the barricades had been taken down the door opened a crack. I widened it with a small shove and a large foot. The unprepossessing face of Leo peered out from the inner gloom.

'What do you want?'

It was clear from his tone that I wasn't going to get it.

'Just a chat. A friendly chat.'

To show how sincere I was, I held the .38 close against his stomach and pushed him back inside.

'L-Listen,' he stammered.

'Shut up. I'll listen in a minute. You got some dead bodies in here?'

The place smelled like a sewage disposal plant.

'Bodies?' he queried.

'Forget it. Those two guys you had

waiting for me last night. Where are they?'

He shook his head and dribbled with fear.

'You got it wrong. I never brought those guys here, I swear. Look, it was Skinny, the guy who cut in yesterday morning. Remember? He was sitting — '

'I know where he was sitting,' I interrupted. 'I know where they were waiting too. In back. And that's not Skinny's territory, is it? That's yours.'

'I couldn't help it. Listen, these are rough people, I couldn't argue with them.'

I waved him back so that he was pressed against the bar counter.

'Where are they?' I repeated.

'I don't know.' He was getting surly now that it seemed I hadn't come to kill him. 'Why don't you ask Skinny.'

'I haven't got Skinny. But I do have you, I'm asking you. I know just what those two did when they left here last night. They gave you a number to call if I ever came in again. Let's have it.'

'I swear — '

I was sick of hearing him swear. I

poked the gun not too gently into his middle. He let out painful air and went a shade greener.

'The number.'

'It's a Paxton number. I'll get it.'

'Try your pockets first. Empty 'em out.'

It was written on a soiled envelope. I put the paper in my pocket.

'What place is it? And don't let's have any more trouble.'

'It's the Pioneer on Twelfth.'

I nodded. Leo, back to the bar, was wishing me dead with his eyes.

'Well, thanks, Leo. You've been a real little pal. Seeing what you did for me last night, I'm going to do something for you. I'm going to tell those monkeys you sent me.'

'You made me, you forced me,' he protested.

'Well, we won't bother them with all the details. So long, Leo. Better watch your back.'

I hadn't thought he could move so fast. Close by his outstretched right hand was a half-filled bottle. He swept this up as I put away the .38 and swung it hard at my head. I got my left arm in the way and got a hefty thump above the elbow. The force knocked the bottle from his hand and it shattered on the floor. My arm hurt.

'That's felonious assault,' I told him. 'You could get up to two years. But today you're lucky. Today we fine you on the spot.'

He came forward with his head down. I stepped to one side and brought by knee up into his face as he charged by. Then I slammed him behind the ear and while he was on his way to the floor I chopped at his neck. He stretched out in the spreading pool of cheap wine, and we weren't going to hear any more about Leo for a while. I went to the wall telephone and damaged the company's property. I didn't know who else Leo might want to call, and I couldn't take any chances.

After that I left him where he was, and drove over to Twelfth Street. The Pioneer must have been a fine place back fifty years ago. You could tell, because they still had the same furniture and decor. Both bore all the marks of half-a-century of use, dirt and tobacco smoke. An aged character peered at me myopically.

'You want a room?' he asked hopefully.

'Sure.'

I put a five dollar bill on the counter and watched it disappear into spidery fingers. Then he heaved a blackbound book towards him, brushing ineffectually at the dust. I put a hand on his arm and shook my head.

'I want a special room,' I explained. 'One that already has two men in it.'

Immediately he was suspicious and afraid. But he was greedy too. I knew the signs.

'Two men? I don't get it. You fuzz or something?'

'Now when did the fuzz ever hand out fins to deserving senior citizens?' I asked him. 'It's just a little private thing. They'll be glad to see me.'

'We ain't got but the one room with two guys in it,' he said hesitantly. 'May not be your friends at all.'

I described Rocky and Smoke and could tell from his face I'd scored.

'Could be them,' he admitted. 'Just might be. But I can't tell you where they

256

are. Those two gentlemen in number seventy-one, they were very particular about not being disturbed. I can't help you, mister. And now I have to go into the office for a coupla minutes.'

He winked evilly and shuffled off. I could be going up there to bump off those characters for all he cared. All he wanted was a quiet life and an occasional five bucks. I knew better than to trust the elevator. It had been one of the very first installed in the city and should have been put out to grass twenty years ago. Instead, I went up the stairs, taking care not to catch my feet in the worn and rotting carpet. Number 71 was on the third floor. Inside I could hear voices, and knew I had the right people. I knocked. At once there was silence inside. I knocked again.

'What do you want?'

Rocky's harsh tones came clearly enough to tell me he was close to the door. I pitched my voice up a few notes.

'Telephone message here from somebody called Leo. He says — '

'Wait. Don't shout it around.'

The door opened. This was my day for

doors. I went through fast, with the .38 leading the way. Rocky stumbled back a pace, glaring murderously. I kicked the door to.

'If that's a gun under there, I'd leave it where it is.'

I was talking to Smoke who had started to dive for the pillow. He froze, and very slowly sat upright.

'Smoke, you get over by that window.'

'Stay where you are. This guy ain't going to do anything.'

To reinforce his words, Rocky turned his back on me slowly and deliberately. Then he went to a chair and sat down. Smoke laughed thinly.

'You can sure figure 'em, Rock. Why don't you blow, stranger?'

His upper arm and shoulder were tightly bandaged. Otherwise he looked mobile enough.

'I'm not through yet,' I replied. 'Rocky's right. I didn't come here to shoot people. I came to talk. But if anybody else wants to start a war, I'd kind of like to be first. Am I reaching you, thin boy?'

He said a word I hadn't heard in years. Rocky helped himself to a cigaret. He was only wearing a shirt and blue pants, and I knew he hadn't a gun on him. That meant I could concentrate on the other one.

'It's your visit. Talk it up,' said Rocky expansively.

'How would you two like to make a deal?'

'Deal,' exploded Smoke. 'What kinda crazy man are you — ?'

'Shut up,' spat Rocky. 'You were saying?'

'You heard me the first time. What's the answer?'

Rocky flicked ash on to the floor and blew gently on the glowing end of his cigaret.

'I once did it myself,' he said reminiscently. 'Stuck one of these against the sole of somebody's foot. It was a woman's foot. What would this deal be about?'

I believed him about the cigaret. It didn't make me love him any more.

'About a certain box. I'll cut you in for one half.'

Smoke trembled with rage, but one look from Rocky convinced him not to start talking.

'Who needs half a box? Is this some kind of double-talk?'

'You need it,' I replied. 'But you haven't got it. You don't even know where it is.'

'Zasso?'

Rocky blew on the butt again and a couple of sparks landed on his pants. He waited for me to talk again, but I could wait too. Finally he looked across.

'About this box,' he began. 'You have it?'

I shook my head.

'If I had it, I wouldn't be here talking deal with a couple of second-raters. I'd be a million miles away.'

Smoke tittered with scorn.

'We'd find you,' he promised. 'If you was ten million miles away.'

'Ha, ha. You can't even find the stuff when it's right in the same city with you.'

The cigaret dropped on the threadbare carpet and Rocky ground it out with great care.

'You're a very mouthy guy, Ballenas.

You got too much to say. And maybe I'll do something about it one day.'

'More talk,' I scoffed. 'Well, if you guys don't want a share, don't say I didn't offer.'

I backed to the door. Smoke looked in quick alarm at the ugly man in the chair.

'Don't just let him walk out. We can't do that.'

I waited to see whether this would have any effect on Rocky. He pushed that fat thumb in his mouth again, staring hard at me.

'Hold it, loudmouth,' he said wearily.

For a man looking at the wrong end of a heavy calibre weapon, Rocky just didn't know his lines.

'Push me too hard and I might forget I don't want to shoot anybody,' I warned.

'Yeah, I'll remember. What's your pitch, buddy boy?'

'I know who's got it. I can't take it by myself. You and the creep here, you help me.'

'Who you calling a creep?' barked Smoke.

'Shuddup,' Rocky whispered. 'The

loudmouth is talking. All right, you. Suppose we help you. What happens then?'

'I already told you. Half for you, half for me,' I repeated.

'You gotta fat nerve. That stuff belongs to us,' said Smoke excitedly.

'No,' I contradicted. 'It doesn't really belong to anybody. Only one man has a real claim, a man named Seldon.'

I didn't bother them with the fact that Seldon had been dead for seven hundred years.

'That's a new one,' Rocky said softly. 'Who's he?'

'Never mind him now. He isn't here. I am, and so are you. Do we have a deal?'

'No,' rejected the ugly man. 'I don't like anything about you. All you have is a lotta nerve and that firing piece. We don't need you. Blow.'

'Rocky, maybe we oughta — '

I never knew whatever it was Smoke thought they oughta. Rocky withered him with one look, and the words strangled in his throat.

'Suit yourself,' I shrugged. 'This way

you get nothing. I'll make my deal some other place.'

'Do that. And don't sit with your back to any doors,' advised Rocky.

Nobody called me back this time. I went out and swung the door shut. In the corridor I waited to see whether anybody wanted to play hero, but there weren't any takers. Then I strolled downstairs to the car.

The traffic wasn't thick, but I stalled around at every signal, every intersection. If there was anybody behind I didn't want to make it tough to follow me. I figured that the two boys wouldn't want to lose sight of me, and I was counting on them.

It was noon as I turned down that quiet road leading to the Meadowlark. There were a few cars around when I parked. There was no friendly young guy in the lobby today. I guess they don't count on too many customers until the evening. There would be just a few of the more regular drinkers on view. I went in the same bar and looked around. Half a dozen men, each one alone, sat nursing their solitary drinks. The bartender looked at me expectantly. He made me wonder what had happened to Ruffino. I winked at him and walked out, making my way to Big Joe Meadows' office.

'My, my, the pretty one comes back.'

Norma leaned against a wall, flexing her muscles and curves in such a way that I wouldn't have any trouble working out what shape she was. Despite the hour, the lady was well into her cups, as they say.

'If you ever stay sober long enough, beautiful, I might do something about you,' I told her.

She fluttered her eyelashes at me. It might have been an effective gesture, only they weren't her eyelashes, and she swayed at the same time.

'Well, that's better,' she mocked. 'I was beginning to wonder if I was getting old.'

'Joe in?'

I thought it was time to cut the fascinating banter. She shrugged with disgust.

'In? The guy is never anywhere else.'

I leered at her in a way she'd understand.

'How about nights?' and I made it

sound as bad as it looked.

She giggled, then looked affronted;

'I tell you the guy never leaves his damned office. He even sleeps in there. Bet you wouldn't sleep in no lousy old office, if there were other places you could be, would you now, honey?'

We were now about ten inches apart, and she contrived to give me a fair overall rubbing with several of those other places. I hadn't realised it was so hot inside the club.

'Not even for you?' I said incredulously.

'Nah. He's never left that crummy room since we came to this lousy town.'

'Four whole months?' I still wasn't convinced.

'And three days,' she confirmed. 'You'd think there'd have to be something wrong with a guy like that, no?'

'Yes.' I admitted. 'I'd think there was.'

I didn't add that I had an idea what the something was.

'I better go see him.'

I made to move away. She insinuated a shoulder in front of me. I didn't mind. She wore a halter bra that wasn't tight

265

enough and red silk shorts.

Only very short. She could rub shoulders with me any time.

'You gonna move in with that creep?' she pouted.

'That's no way to talk about your loving husband,' I chided.

'He's — '

She stopped as soon as she began.

'He's what, honey?'

I stroked a thoughtful finger along one bronzed shoulder. She shuddered and closed her eyes.

'What is he, old Joe?' I queried.

'Let's forget about Joe,' she murmured. 'How long will you be?'

'Not too long. You go wait in the bar. And take it easy with that stuff. We don't want anybody falling asleep, huh?'

She chuckled lazily.

'Don't worry, pretty boy. I think I'll stick to ginger ale for a while. If you think it's worth it.'

'I'll have to let you decide that,' I told her. 'A little later.'

'Not too much later. I have a helluva thirst,' she warned.

266

Then she uncoiled herself and took off in the general direction of the bar. I had a feeling I was being watched and looked quickly at the nearest window. I could be wrong, but I fancied there was a blur of movement there, just as my head turned. I went to Meadows' office, turned the handle and walked in. He looked up in surprise from a racing sheet.

'You got your nerve busting in here,' he said calmly. 'Bust out again whenever you're ready.'

'Got something for you, Joe.'

I tossed an envelope on the desk in front of him. He looked at it, puzzled. Then he put down the paper and picked up the envelope. He peeked inside.

'What's this?' he demanded.

'What it looks like,' I replied. 'Five hundred bucks.'

'What's it for?'

'It's the same five hundred you gave me last night. I'm handing it back.'

In Joe's world people don't hand money around once they have their hands on it. Come to think of it, Joe's world wasn't different from anybody else's world.

'Handing it — back?' he questioned.

'Sure. I said I'd do what I could to keep the boys in blue out of your joint. Just because some of your boys got mixed up in something outside, that was no reason you should have a lot of interference in your business. That was what you said.'

'So? You figured it was a fair deal last night.'

'A lot's happened since last night,' I replied.

'A lot of what's happened?'

'Mind if I sit down?'

I parked where I could see both windows. Meadows' face was a mask.

'Shakedown, huh?' he snapped. 'How much more do you want?'

I shook my head.

'I never shake people down. The money you gave me last night was a fair price. You wouldn't have heard any more from me. The reason I brought back your dough is I can't keep the law away. In fact I'm going to bring them here myself.'

'Ah.'

It was a very small utterance but there was a wealth of menace behind it.

'Yes,' I confirmed. 'I'm afraid you weren't quite straight with me, Joe. The little guy, Ruffino, that was quite a show you put on here for me last night. Of course, at the time I didn't know the man was doing what you told him to do.'

He clasped powerful hands in front of his face.

'What did I tell him to do?'

'What he did do. Hand out the bait to Reuben Adler.'

'You're crazy.'

'Uh, uh,' I denied. 'Maybe a little slow on the uptake, but not crazy. That was a nice stunt you pulled last night. With the little guy out of the way there wouldn't be any need for people to come around asking nasty questions about boxes.'

'You said boxes?' he asked in apparent disbelief.

'Just one box, I imagine. Where've you got it, by the way?'

He leaned back and his hands went out of sight. He chuckled.

'Talk. Just words. You got nothing to play with. Nothing at all.'

'Oh, yes I do. I have Thompson.'

He looked puzzled.

'You remember Sam Thompson,' I chided. 'Your boys worked him over last night.'

'Did they? What did he do?' was the innocent question.

It was my turn to grin.

'You don't give up easy, do you Joe? I called Sam from this club. Between that time and the time he was taken, I never mentioned his name to a living soul.'

'So what does that prove?'

'The phone,' I explained. 'You probably have somebody monitoring every call that goes out of this place. It would explain something else, too.'

'Like what?'

'Like the reason somebody else hasn't been able to make a call from here at all. That one had me worried till now. The place is littered with phones, and I thought it would be easy to make a call. But of course, if you don't like what's being said, the phone goes dead.'

He moved his great weight into a more comfortable position. I wished I could see his hands.

'Preston, you are liable to say something that makes me mad if you ain't careful,' he warned.

'I'll have it in mind.'

'All this crap about phones, where does it get us? Nothing you've said bothers me so far. Why don't you go fly a kite?'

'I can't stand heights. And the stuff about the phones is no crap. As you well know. Come to think about it, there's a serious charge right there. I'm sure the telephone company would prosecute. Tinkering with company property.'

'Lay off,' he advised. 'Talk about something serious.'

'All right, how about the demise of one McKern?'

His face went very tense.

'What about it?'

'I think we can pin that on you, Joe.'

There was something like relief in his voice when he said,

'Then try, brother. I don't know the first thing about it. And you can't

271

produce a single fact that even connects me with McKern, leave alone to say I bumped him off.'

It was my turn to say 'Ah'.

'Ah,' and I wagged a finger for emphasis. 'But I can, Joe. I can produce enough evidence connecting you with McKern to make it seem very likely you had good reasons to get rid of him. And the police will like the way I set it out.'

'Crazy man,' he scoffed. 'You got nothing. I didn't even know the jerk had been knocked off until — '

He stopped talking as though his voice had run out of battery.

'Go ahead, Joe,' I invited. 'Until when?'

'Until I heard it over the radio,' he finished lamely.

I was feeling more confident now. I was guessing a good part of the time from the meagre stock of facts I'd built up. But I was picking up good cards as the game progressed.

'And I suppose that wasn't your boys dumped McKern in the bay?'

'I told you,' he said carefully. 'None of my people rubbed him out.'

'Sure, you told me. But you didn't say it wasn't your boys put him in the water. And I think it was.'

'You oughta see a doctor. What do you think I am? I'm in business to dump other people's kills?'

'This one, yes.'

'Mind telling me why?'

I hadn't taken my eyes away from the windows much, but it was a little worrying trying to watch Meadows at the same time.

'You have to go back a little, back several months. It seems there's a long-lost treasure down in Baja California. Suddenly it might not be lost any more, and people get very interested. All kinds of people. The main bunch are some fellows from Yuma, and one of those is McKern.'

Meadows held up a hand to stifle a yawn. But he was listening.

'The Yuma brigade are tough enough for whatever they have to do. But this so-called treasure is a little out of the usual run. A lot of the stuff consists of old gold pieces, and none of these boys knows a thing about that kind of merchandise. But they have to know what it is they're buying or more likely stealing. So they get an expert. A guy who's not got any kind of record. This guy can use the money because he has this sister who's all kinds of a lush, to say the least of it. The chance of several thousand quick dollars is something the poor devil's dreamed about. So they put it to him, and he agrees. Do I hold your interest?'

'Go ahead,' he said dreamily. 'I got nothing else to do right now. Let me know when you're through. I want you to meet some friends of mine.'

'Love it, maybe some of my friends will join us, too.'

He was less dreamy at once.

'More talk,' he decided. 'You don't have any friends. Unless you count Thompson and I guess — '

For the second time he could have bitten off his tongue.

'That's right, Joe,' I nodded. 'You guess Thompson won't be bothering anybody for a while because of the beating he took last night.'

Big Joe shrugged.

'Ah, what's the diff.? You ain't gonna be telling anybody.'

'We'll see. Let me tell you about these guys from Yuma. They go after this old piggy-bank and they find it. I don't know the details, but I guess the police down there in Baja can fill those in. Meanwhile, back at the ranch, things are happening. Another outfit gets to hear the story. I don't know how and it doesn't matter. They don't want a shooting war with Yuma, so they play it cool. They grab the girl, the alcoholic sister of the expert, and take it from there. Maybe they made a deal with McKern, or maybe he just horned in, it doesn't matter. What matters is that McKern and Austin, that's the expert I was telling you about, they blow with the magic box and come to Monkton City. They come to you, Joe. And you know the rest of it.'

He tutted and inspected me shrewdly.

'You know, Preston, I can't figure you. What you been telling me, you worked all that out from square one. That's pretty good, in my book. That would make you smart, and I don't say that to many people.'

I half-bowed, still keeping one eye on the windows. Meadows wasn't finished.

'Up to there, that's smart. I can figure all kinds of angles you could play from there. So what do you do? You come bustin' in here alone, give me back my five hundred, tell me the whole story. That ain't smart, Preston. That ain't even half-smart. That is plain dumb.'

He must have pushed some kind of signal without me seeing. The door opened suddenly and two men came in. They had restless eyes and watchful faces. I didn't know them, but the breed was familiar. Under my arm the .38 felt comfortable and friendly, but a long way off. All I could count on was the tiny single shot derringer which was strapped to my wrist. And one small slug against three large men is not the kind of odds I like to play.

'Well, well.' Meadows sounded surprised. 'My friends are here. Where are your friends, Preston?'

The man was right, I didn't have any

friends. But I did have two murderous characters lurking around outside who might do something for my good without meaning to. I looked sickly.

'Maybe it was a dumb thing to do,' I admitted.

'You can bet on it,' Meadows assured me.

'What's the action, boss?'

The nearer of Meadows' friends had a voice like a chicken disappearing down a fox's throat. But there didn't seem to be much else about him that would be chicken. The man behind the desk pointed a stubby finger at me.

'This guy's been working too hard. He needs a rest.'

The two looked at me dispassionately.

'A long rest?' queried Chicken Throat.

'Yeah. A very long rest. I'm sorry, Preston, we coulda got along, but you see how it is. A man has to protect his investments.'

I stood up.

'A man usually gets a last request.'

'What are you, kidding?' he snapped. 'What do you want, reporters?'

'No. Just a look at the box. I know it's in the office here. Not much to ask, is it?'

'Come on, you, we're wasting time,' squeaked the man nearest me.

'Ah, what the hell. He's right, it ain't much. I'm feeling bad about him anyway.'

Meadows went to the wall and swung back a picture to reveal a small safe. I thought that went out with the Model-T Ford. He fiddled with the combination and swung back the door. The opening was very small and I felt disappointment. When his hand came out it held only a key. Meadows grinned.

'Neat, huh? It would take an expert thirty minutes to open that safe. Every alarm in the place would be sounding all hell. And when he gets inside, all he gets is this.'

He shifted a silver ashtray on the table. Underneath it was a keyhole into which he inserted the key. The whole top of the table slid soundlessly to one side and he dived into the space beneath. With two hands he carefully raised a wooden casket bound with strips of black metal that might have been brass once. I took a step

278

forward but something hard and familiar jabbed into my side.

'Just take it easy. And we'll take any hardware now.'

I raised my arms high and a searching hand slid inside my coat. The man gave a small grunt of satisfaction as he located the .38 and pulled it out. I would have started some heroics then, but the other one was all of six feet clear of me. He would have had time to empty two guns into me before I could reach him. And the look on his face told me it would be a pleasure.

'He's clean, Joe.'

'Let him come take a look.'

I went up close. Meadows tapped gently at the carved lid of the box.

'Beautiful, ain't it?'

Despite myself, I couldn't help a strange feeling as I looked at it. I thought about what Adler had told me. I thought about knights in armour, swarthy pirates, Spanish men-at-arms and the whole colorful history of the box. In museums these things don't always have that impact on me. But this was here, this was for real. And after seven centuries, people were double-dealing and killing for it. Some of those old-timers must be laughing in their graves. Big Joe carefully raised the lid. There were a few stones, mostly pearls, otherwise the box was jammed with coins.

'Don't look much to me,' I commented.

Meadows stroked at the box almost delicately.

'Nobody cares what you think. You're all washed up. Well, you've seen it. Use the side entrance.'

'C'm on, you.'

Meadows didn't look up as I turned to go. We were at the door. Squeaky Voice said,

'Don't start nothin' out there.'

I shrugged. He opened the door and went first. There was a crash of breaking glass and the roar of a gun. I hit the floor hard as my two companions wheeled round. Big Joe was sinking to the ground holding his side. Rocky was standing at the window, smoke curling from the snout of an automatic. Rocky fired again and the second man screamed as he clutched a ruined shoulder. Squeaky had a gun levelled. I grabbed his ankle and yanked him over. The gun went off, a bullet spanging harmlessly into the ceiling. Rocky couldn't sight us easily on the floor. He ducked down out of view. As Squeaky grounded I chopped him hard at the side of the neck and he lay still. I grabbed up the gun and bellied forward to the protection of the big desk. Outside people were shouting.

'Keep away from the door,' I cried.

Somebody didn't hear me. There were rushing feet, then another shot from the window. Whoever it was at the door yelled either with pain or fear, and got out of range.

'There's two of them outside,' I yelled. 'Get the police. Meadows is dead.'

Voices arguing, but I didn't pay them any attention. I had enough trouble right where I was. Inching to the corner of the desk I stuck one eye quickly round. I pulled it back fast as Rocky let fly, and a large sliver of wood whizzed past my ear. I was worried about Smoke, and what he was up to. Then I decided to try an old jungle tactic. I checked the gun, a heavy old-fashioned .45, and found there were six slugs in it. Next I got close to the corner and pointed the gun at the angle the window should be. When I was satisfied I took a deep breath. Suddenly I poked the gun round and fired in an arc four times. The angle must have been good, three of the shots hit glass. On the fourth shot I brought my head round too. The window was empty. It didn't have to mean I'd hit Rocky. No sane man is going to stand still against a roving spray of lead. But it did mean I could get clear of the table.

I came out fast and flattened myself against the wall by the window. There were only two bullets left in the .45 and I wasn't going to get any second chances. If I got very lucky that would be one each for Rocky and Smoke, but I didn't pin too much faith in that kind of luck. It wasn't all that hot, but I was sweating violently. If I didn't know myself better, I would have said that was fear. It was time Rocky made a play. Edging along the wall, I came level with the window. The noise out in the passage had stopped, and the only familiar sound was that fast thudding in my chest. Then I could hear something else, the heavy laboured breathing of a man outside the window. I froze where I was. Suddenly, a foot from me, the wicked nose of the automatic poked through the broken glass. I swung the .45 down hard and there was a shout of pain as the force of the blow knocked the gun clear of Rocky's grasp and into the room. I scooped it up from the floor and looked outside. Rocky stood there nursing a bleeding wrist. As the blow forced the automatic downwards it had also jabbed his wrist on to the jagged glass of the window. There was a dark stain high up on his left arm too, so I must have hit him with one of the spray shots.

'Where's Smoke?'

He told me to go somewhere. I threw open the window.

'Get in here. Or would you like me to help?'

He hesitated then clambered painfully

through. Ignoring me, he went straight to the desk and looked at the box. It was the only time I ever saw real emotion on his face.

'All that trouble,' he muttered. 'All those people.'

'Let's talk about people,' I suggested. 'Where's Smoke?'

Reluctantly, he looked away from the box. The face he turned towards me could have been made of stone.

'You was the error,' he said calmly. 'I shoulda let Smoke take you that first time.'

'He might still do it if you don't tell me where he is.'

Rocky smiled malevolently.

'Yeah, I know. That's all I got to hold on to.'

I called to the people outside.

'Get in here. It's all over.'

Murmuring at the door, then the young college-looking guy came in, followed by Austin. They stared at the three men on the ground, then at Rocky.

'He won't bite. I just took his teeth out.'

I waved the ugly man's automatic, then threw it on the desk. From the prostrate Squeaky Voice I recovered my own gun.

'You people call any cops?' I demanded.

The young one shook his head.

'No. Mr. Meadows wouldn't want us to do that.'

I nodded as though I'd expected it, picked up the phone on the table and dialled. I stood where I could see them all, and they could see the .38.

'You guys have to get used to some new thinking around here. What Meadows wants or doesn't want doesn't matter any more. It's what the police want.'

'Is — is he really dead?'

There was more hope than sympathy in Austin's enquiry.

'He's either dead or close to it,' I replied. 'Hallo, Police?'

I was put through to Randall. Quickly I told him what had happened. I also told him who was still standing up as I phoned. Austin and the campus kid looked at each other quickly. I put down the receiver.

'That's so you got a lot to explain if

anything unusual happens here the next few minutes. Here, you.'

Austin looked surprised as I handed him Rocky's gun.

'If this mug so much as breathes too hard, let him have it. And do it right the first time. There won't be any second chances with this baby.'

The ex-manager, ex-coin expert stared at the weapon.

'I don't quite understand. Are you leaving?'

I pointed to Rocky.

'Buddy-boy here has a friend outside. If I don't find him quick he's going to kill me some dark night.'

Rocky chuckled.

'That you can bet on.'

I went out through the window after a quick glance around. Outside I got down to a crouch, wondering where to start. It seemed likely Smoke would have gone around to the other window, so he and Rocky could attack from different positions. The only question was, why hadn't Smoke started anything? Uncomfortably aware that I'd exhausted my supply of luck for one day, I crouch-walked towards the corner of the building, expecting any moment to hear a chuckle from behind. Then I peered cautiously round.

He was lying sideways on the ground, back arched forward. One hand, his good one, had frozen in its position of trying to pluck from his back a slender black knife, murderously and accurately home. There wasn't any chuckle. All I heard was a faint swish of air as somebody drove a truck into the side of my head. I tried a mouthful of the local dust. Dimly aware that I mustn't lose consciousness, I fought against the inviting red mist that swirled and beckoned in front of my eyes. Somewhere a gun went off as I struggled to my knees. The .38 lay a couple of feet away. I tried to pick it up, but they make them very heavy these days. There was more noise, people shouting, a car motor. I tried another grab at the gun, made it this time. Clambering awkwardly to my feet I took a manly pace forward and felt my face crunch against the side of the building. I held on to the smooth stone and counted to ten. Next try I made it to the window. College boy had the gun now, and Austin was cradling a bleeding hand. Rocky hadn't moved. They all saw me at once.

'The box, he took the box,' yelled the young one.

'Who did?' I snarled.

'Never saw him before. He shot Mr. Austin in the hand, grabbed up the box and ran. We didn't have a chance.'

'All right. Police be here soon. Watch that one.'

I had tried to say more, but only odd words came out. At some kind of shambling lope I got to the Chev and climbed in. One thing was for sure. If a cop stopped me on the road I was a cinch for a drunk driving rap, the state I was in.

11

The first time I went to the Adler house I thought it had been built for a horror movie. The house hadn't changed this trip, and it seemed appropriate there should be a long-lost treasure inside it. I recognised the car that was parked out front. The drive had cleared my head, except for a throbbing ache. I pulled up well clear of the house, and walked the rest of the way. It was no time for visiting cards at the big front door. I took a chance Adler would use the same room where he'd received me. Soon I was peeking through a big open window.

Juan Miguel Gilbert Ballenas looked as immaculate as ever, but his voice was excited. Adler sat watching him with every evidence of composure.

'Señor Adler, I know you to be a man of great distinction, and of course a man of business. If you wish to bargain with me over the price, then perhaps I could see my way to a small reduction. To be frank, señor, I do not have enough time to bargain properly. I will settle for one hundred thousand, paid now.'

Adler shook his head. In front of him, the open box had spilled a few coins. It never looked more like something from the Spanish Main.

'I assure you, señor, I am not one to bargain when there is something I want. And I wanted what was in this box very much. But this,' he picked up a handful of coins disdainfully and ran them through his fingers. 'This is junk, sir. Comparative junk. At a rough guess, and if you could find a dealer who could be bothered with it, you might get six — no perhaps seven hundred dollars for the lot.'

Ballenas just wasn't able to believe him.

'Seven hundred dollars?' he echoed. 'But, señor, men have died — who can tell how many men have died? And for — this? For this seven hundred dollar pile of waste?'

Again the older man shook his head.

'No, sir. Men have died, certainly, but not for this. This is not Seldon's Gold.'

The Spaniard's face grew crafty.

'Then, señor, you will have no objection if I take the box with me?'

'None at all, sir. If you consider it worth having.'

I could have kept quiet. But I knew Adler had the purchase money somewhere in the house. For all I could tell, Ballenas might know it, too. And he might decide to take it along with him for consolation. I just didn't feel able to let him do that. So I walked in letting Ballenas see the .38 plain and clear. He made a face and shrugged.

'You have the head like iron, Señor Preston.'

'Preston? What is the meaning of this?'

Adler tried to sound pompous, but it came out empty.

'Sorry I didn't knock. But this is a very strange visitor you have here. If I hadn't shown my face, you might have been a lot poorer in ten minutes time.'

The old man looked quickly at the Spaniard, who smiled widely.

'There is the matter of my expenses, you understand?'

'Was,' I corrected. 'There is now only the matter of what to do with you.'

'Would you mind telling me what this is all about?' said Adler testily.

He was talking to me. I looked at him, and I didn't feel friendly.

'Did you ask him that?' I waved the gun at Ballenas.

'Eh? No, of course I didn't. He's only been here a matter of minutes.'

'I only just walked in,' I pointed out. 'But you're asking me.'

'I am, and getting no answer. What is your point, Preston?'

'My point is,' I explained slowly, 'that there is a difference between this man and myself. When he came, he brought the box. And that took care of the questions. All that mattered was the box.'

'You have no right to question me — ' spluttered Adler.

'You'll take it from me or the police, as you choose. Did you ask the Spanish gentleman whether he murdered anybody to get this?'

The old man went very still.

'No, of course you didn't. You don't

care what he did. All that mattered was the box.'

'The thing is worthless,' intoned Adler.

'Sure, I heard you. So now you can build up a whole new attitude to it. But people have died. A man was killed this morning, maybe two. I don't suppose you want to be told that?'

He stared at the floor and wouldn't look up.

'There have always been people like you. The ones with the money bags. You don't want to hear about what goes on in the dirty world outside. Don't want to be told about the grime and the blood, the trouble caused by things like this box. If things look like getting close to home, you can always rent out somebody like me to go out and take your lumps.'

He raised the white head and regarded me levelly.

'Is that not your profession?'

'It is. But there's nothing in the rules says I have to like the client. Don't worry, this thing is cleaned up now. A few people have been shot, stabbed, beaten up. I won't bother you with the sordid side of the thing. Just the bill.'

'And an explanation of what happened.'

'That too. It's part of the service I keep the law off your back as much as possible. You'll get the full service. First I have to get rid of him.'

Adler was alarmed at once.

'I couldn't possibly countenance — '

'Don't worry, I don't mean kill him. I mean get him where he can't hear what I tell you.'

Ballenas showed me all his teeth.

'I am much relieved, señor. I did not think you would repay in such an offhand way, but people are always surprising me, I regret to say.'

I turned to Adler.

'I want this guy locked up. You and I have a lot to talk about before we send for the police. Is there a cellar maybe?'

'Yes. I'll show you.'

He led us to an old-fashioned heavy cellar door.

'Not much down there these days,' said Adler. 'But there is a light. The key is here.'

'Thanks. I'll see to him and come back.'

The white-haired man looked at each of us in turn then walked away.

'All right, you. Inside,' I said gruffly.

Ballenas shrugged and went in. I followed him down dusty steps. At the bottom I said,

'What happened with Smoke?'

'Smoke?'

'The man you knifed at the Meadowlark.'

'That one. I regretted having to do that, believe me. But he was going to kill you. There were two of them, both with guns. I had no guns, señor, so I could not fight them both in the open. While you were shooting at one man, this other, this Smoke, he went to the other window. He could not have failed to kill you. This I could not allow.'

I looked at the bland face.

'Why?' I demanded.

'Because we are the partners,' was the astonished reply.

'H'm. And what about later, when you clunked me over the head? Was that because we're partners, too?'

He shrugged, and the well-cut jacket complained.

'But of course not. That was a matter of money. In matters of life and death I am your partner. But in matters of money, señor, one has to be a realist. I could have killed you just as easy, but this would be unforgivable.'

To him it made sense. And, knowing the man, to me, too. I grinned.

'And what about this so-called client of yours, Señor Vicente? You were all set to double-cross him over the box.'

'A decision I took with much regret, believe me. I could get the box, yes. But I would never get it out of the country. For your police, I have much respect. So I thought at least I would dispose of the stuff to my profit.'

'And now what?'

Again the jacket heaved.

'That is for you to say, señor. It seems you have the advantage.'

I looked at this man whose mother had been infatuated with an old movie star. The man who had saved my life certainly once, possibly twice.

'You're an expert on old movies,' I told him. 'I'm trying to remember a title, maybe you can help. This guy, the hero, he gets trapped by the bad boys in an old country house. They lock him in the cellar, leave the key in the door. Now this hero character, he pushed the key out of the lock so it fell on the carpet outside the door. Then he carefully pulled the carpet towards him till he could reach the key and let himself out. You remember that movie?'

He flashed a relieved smile.

'I regret, señor, that I do not. What did such a hero use to push out the key?'

'You know these heroes, they always have something around. Maybe he had a knife, a thin-bladed knife? That would have done it.'

'Ah, yes,' he nodded emphatically. 'Now I remember, it was such a knife.'

I turned to go.

'Well, I can't stand around chewing old movies with a desperate character like you. I'm going to lock you down here till the police come. Is that clear?'

'Very clear, señor. Muyos gracias.'

I went up the stairs. At the top I waved, and he flipped me a mock salute. I made a lot of noise locking the door. Back in Adler's room, he said,

'Is everything all right?'

'He's safe enough. It'd take three men to bust down that door.'

'Good. We must send for the police at once.'

'Hold on, Mr. Adler. They have their hands full at the Meadowlark. Another ten minutes will make no difference to the police, but it'll be a great help to us. Let me tell you what happened.'

I told him all the facts he needed to know. It wouldn't be smart to tell him everything, because soon he would be talking to Rourke. When people talk to the big Irishman they usually wind up telling everything they know, whether they're aware of it or not.

'A dreadful story, dreadful,' muttered Adler. 'But I don't understand how things got so far. I mean, surely once the man Austin had seen this stuff, the thing need have gone no further?'

'That would be the obvious result,' I agreed. 'The truth of that will come out now. But for my guess, Austin was in too deep by the time he reached the box. Remember the kind of people he was with, dangerous people. They'd been to a lot of trouble to get the box, spent money. They didn't take Austin down there just so he could tell them they were holding junk. Plus, he may then have known his sister had been grabbed by Meadows. The only way to get her free was to produce the box. And a box full of worthless coins is no way to try paying off a man like Meadows. You have to remember Austin is not really a criminal character. Just an ordinary kind of joe who was picked up by some very nasty people. He wouldn't be equipped to deal with them.'

Adler nodded, and looked at me thoughtfully.

'But the first three coins?' he asked. 'The noble, the bezant, the doubloon? No doubt about their authenticity, none whatever.'

'There can be only two answers to that,' I replied. 'And the devil of it is, if

Austin won't talk, we may never know which is correct.'

'Only two, you say? What are those?'

There was a sudden noise of a car motor outside. I had a quiet grin, but kept it inside my face. Adler heard it too, but he couldn't be bothered with mundane matters. He was waiting to hear what I had to say.

'First explanation, the coins came out of the box. That box,' I pointed. 'If so, the chances are it is the genuine Vicente box.'

'But the rest,' protested Adler. 'Where is the rest?'

'I'll have to pass on that,' I confessed. 'After three centuries, the stuff is probably scattered far and wide throughout Mexico. Maybe the Indians used the coins to make arrowheads, the stones to decorate their women's bodies.'

Adler shuddered at the prospect. He didn't like the first explanation at all.

'And the other solution?' he demanded eagerly.

'The coins were used to salt the box. How much would they be worth?'

'Oh, quite a lot. I haven't bothered to

check, but quite a thousand dollars. Quite that.'

'Well, that would be a fair investment, wouldn't it? Once Austin had taken the plunge, he'd have to keep it up. Those three probably came from his own collection for the sole purpose of deceiving you.'

'Much more likely. Far more likely.'

Adler didn't know whether it was more likely or not. He didn't care. All he cared about was to preserve the legend of Seldon's Gold. If the box in front of him was Vicente's box, it was the end of the legend. No, the second idea had to be right, he decided.

'You know, that's the one thing that still puzzles me. How did these people expect me to pay over all that money for this rubbish? I'm not quite a fool, and they must know it.'

'You're forgetting they didn't know it was junk,' I reminded. 'And in any case it would have made no difference to your paying over the money. You may be no fool, Mr. Adler, but you're no criminal either. You'd have been no match for those guys once they got within spending distance of your money.'

'You're probably right. Well, shall we call the police?'

'First, shall we clear my bill, Mr. Adler. You may find it expensive, and certainly you get no return.'

He opened a drawer and took out a metal box, the same one from which he'd paid me last time.

'A pleasure, Mr. Preston. As to any return, I think I will take some consolation from the fact that you've almost certainly saved me one hundred thousand dollars, and not impossibly my life.'

He started sorting bills. The door was opened with a rush, and into the room burst the tall silver blonde who was Pauline Adler. She was surprised to see me.

'Oh, you're here,' she said without pleasure. 'Father, who was your idiot friend, the one who just left?'

Adler frowned.

'Pauline, I've told you before, I will not have you coming into this room without ceremony. And what are you babbling

302

about? No one has been here but Mr. Preston.'

'A dark, good-looking man,' she insisted. 'Nearly forced me off the road as he swung out of the place.'

'Ballenas,' I snapped, leaving the room at a run.

The cellar door stood open, the key on the inside. I inspected the lock carefully, and was pleased to see my thoughtful friend had made several deep new scratches. That would bear out my story to the police. It was his ball now, and I somehow felt he'd make it over the border. When I got back to the others, Adler was showing his daughter the box.

'He's got away,' I said tersely. 'Must get the police at once, Mr. Adler, please.'

He nodded and picked up the telephone. Pauline Adler planted herself in front of me, and she did not look pleased. Diving in her purse, she came out with an official-looking paper and waved it at me.

'Do you know what this is?'

'Looks like a summons,' I offered.

'It is. Do you know what for?'

'Obtaining entry under false pretences?' I suggested. 'Or whatever the correct words are?'

'Whatever the correct words are, that is what it means,' she confirmed.

'How dare you take out a summons against me?'

'How dare you take out a summons against me?' I echoed.

She chewed the inside of her cheek.

'But that was different,' she insisted. 'I hadn't any intention of pressing that charge.'

'You took out the summons just the same,' I pointed out. 'This way, we sort of cancel each other out wouldn't you say? We ought to be capable of a more satisfactory relationship than this.'

Her eyes twinkled.

'You're a cool devil.'

'I get warmer in the evenings,' I explained. 'Let's do the show again tonight. You come round and force your way in, and I'll wrestle with you. But no summons.'

She looked at me appraisingly, then suddenly chuckled.

'I might do that.'

I thought she might, too.

Adler put down the telephone.

'The police are on their way.'

No more treasure now. No more galleons, knights, pirates. No more Aztecs, Spanish gold, dreams of lost fortunes. Just, the police are on their way.

That's how it always ends.

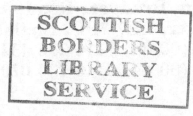